VIGIL

STORIES

SUSIE
TAYLOR

Breakwater Books
PO Box 2188, St. John's, NL, Canada, A1C 6E6
www.breakwaterbooks.com

A CIP catalogue record for this book is available from Library and Archives Canada.

ISBN 978-1-77853-0203 (softcover)

© 2024 Susie Taylor

All rights reserved. No part of this publication may be reproduced, stored in a retrieval system or transmitted, in any form or by any means, without the prior written consent of the publisher or a licence from The Canadian Copyright Licensing Agency (Access Copyright). For an Access Copyright licence, visit www.accesscopyright.ca or call toll free 1-800-893-5777.

We acknowledge the support of the Canada Council for the Arts. We acknowledge the financial support of the Government of Canada through the Department of Heritage and the Government of Newfoundland and Labrador through the Department of Tourism, Culture, Arts and Recreation for our publishing activities.

Printed and bound in Canada.

Breakwater Books is committed to choosing papers and materials for our books that help to protect our environment. To this end, this book is printed on a recycled paper and other sources that are certified by the Forest Stewardship Council®.

Canada Council for the Arts Conseil des Arts du Canada

For Colleen

CONTENTS

BAY MAL VERDE

~

Bay Mal Verde loves all her children. Her children have been delinquents and debutants, magistrates, and more usefully, mechanics. She has even adopted a few poet paupers and given them shelter. There was a pirate, one of her favourites, despite his obvious anger issues. And she produced a premier, although she always felt he was more his father's child. There was a time when she herself was meant for greater things, until that sister of hers, St. John's, started fluttering around and luring away all her suitors. Bay Mal Verde was left with a cathedral that sat on her hand like the engagement ring from a called-off wedding. Expensive to insure with little resale value.

Her current brood is suffering, and she sees it. She doesn't feed them well; they live off cheap white bread and hope. Her grocery stores have shut down, and there isn't even a bus she can stick them on if they need a trip to the doctor's. Her kids run wild, and she finds it hard to keep track of their needs and desires. Too many of them are slipping through the cracks. She says her organs are failing, her spine too buckled to pick them up and nurse them. "I am too old for all this," she moans. Still, she feels a twinge of guilt as she watches addiction creep and potential fail. Her cousins laugh, what do you know of age? Damascus huffs. Aleppo shakes her tired head, what do you know of trouble? But Bay Mal Verde ignores them like the white North American teenager she is. She claims geriatric pregnancy, claims that she is in failing health, that she can't be any help to her current brood and their various predilections. Although, this is not entirely true, she has moments when she redeems herself, lashes out and slaps back a baby's cherubic hand reaching towards a hot glowing coal in the fireplace.

Her personal profile says she is looking for love, but all the hits she gets are looking for one-night stands. St. John's tells her to hang in there, you go girl, be your best self, things can change. Look at their sister Fogo, they had all but forgotten she existed, but a little make-over and now she's the famous one, getting all the attention from magazines and visits from dignitaries arriving in helicopters, not because of natural disaster, but just to have dinner with her.

"Fuck that," says Bay Mal Verde, because she doesn't want those privileged politicians and American actresses demanding spa treatments and vegan meals. She will stay as she is, in her crumbling glory, occasionally entertaining her kids by pulling out some illegal fireworks and setting them off in the middle of the night. And St. John's, she is always having to reinvent herself so she can keep up with the times. Not Bay Mal Verde, she is done with facelifts and self-improvement. Bay Mal Verde will let her rosacea show, she will glory in the lines on the backs of her hands, get herself a fancy cane to help her out when she struggles with gout and arthritis. She won't age gracefully; she will crumble and burn and make everyone a little uncomfortable with her obvious decline. She will be like one of those aging rock stars who gets drunk and stumbles around the stage forgetting the words to her hit songs.

Sometimes she sleeps for weeks, lets the snow blanket her, or allows herself to be slowly sedated by creeping fog. When she comes to, she shakes herself a little, looks around and assesses the damage. She counts her missing, reads the funeral notices that have gone up during her slumber. Then she sends out howling winds. This is how she mourns her dead. She shakes the houses in her rage, brings rocks crumbling down cliffsides. Her children hear her then, remember she is in charge despite her bouts of depression. She will be all tough love with them for a while, their absent mother returned in a manic fit of matriarchal concern, threatening to whip or expel them if they don't get their acts together. But they know it is all bluster. Soon she will tire, pretend she doesn't notice them sneaking cigarettes behind the gas station or the growing bellies of her supposedly virginal daughters.

VIGIL

~

All that is left of the impromptu memorial at the Ultramar is one rosary tied around the cage for the propane tanks. Gary Coombs felt a stab of regret the day he went in early, earlier than ever before, to clear away the wind-tattered ribbons, the bows, the plastic flowers, the water-soaked and mildewed teddy bears, and the sodden and faded packs of cigarettes (Canadian Classics, Stevie's preferred brand). Other offerings were discreetly removed almost as soon as they were left. Someone had stuck a whole untouched Happy Meal on the growing pile of tributes, with a note, a heart-shaped Post-it with *Stevie* scrawled on it in a kid's handwriting, and the gulls swarmed the thing. And there was the booze. A couple of young guys came by and left big showy bottles of Lamb's. Kev Babcock had left a bottle of Crown Royal in a purple bag. Gary couldn't have that stuff out for the taking in front of the store. He gave the bottles to Stevie's mom, Arlene. He told Brenda that's what he was doing; her son Carter had left one of the 26ers. Gary knew she'd pass the information on to Carter, and he'd let the other boys know.

The day Gary cleared it all up, he worked fast, bagging everything and putting it in the dumpster. High winds were expected later and, already, bits of the black-and-purple ribbon wreaths people had hung on their doors in honour of Stevie were blowing through the streets of the town. Gary kept the tiny toy ATV someone had left and stuck it on top of the collection tin they kept at the cash. It was a fund for Stevie's headstone. A metal coffee can with a coin slot cut in its plastic lid. It wasn't filling fast. No one used cash these days, but Brenda had come in to work excitedly a few days ago to tell Gary someone had made a big anonymous donation on GoFundMe. "Enough for something real nice," she'd said, and nodded. "Who was it, I wonder?" Brenda then reeled off some ideas: a local who'd won gold in the Olympics, the town's one NHL star, or the musician from that band in St. John's. The one who'd quit drinking and was always "paying it forward," picking up people's bills at Tim Hortons and the Dollar Store.

Stevie's not the first to go missing around here. The woods, the ocean, can take a person and never give them back. At first, people speculated that Stevie stowed away on a ship and was living in Norway. Maybe he'd been kidnapped and held as a sex slave in some cabin in the woods, or maybe he'd gone feral, living off berries and trapping rabbits.

The day Stevie's disappearance made the news, the town organized a vigil. His mom, Arlene, hadn't contacted the cops until he was gone for three days, figuring he was on a bender. The police, well, they knew Stevie, and it took them a while to start looking. Arlene hadn't seen Stevie for a week by the time the search got serious.

The vigil was candle-lit but with no open flames (too dangerous). Attendees were encouraged to either bring a battery-lit candle or download the "mourning flame" app on their phones, a perpetual flickering image of a candle that never shrank down or got blown out. The vigil was well attended. Brenda went with her daughter Evie, who sobbed through the whole thing, which surprised Brenda. Brenda guessed Evie's period was coming.

Fourteen-year-old Britany Dawe, one of Stevie's cousins, sang "Ode to Newfoundland" and Reverend Hynes, who has a church in his basement called Redemption Faith Centre, prayed loudly and evangelically for Stevie's return. Arlene got up to speak. Rev. Hynes put his arm around her shoulders and led her to the front of the crowd, but she was sobbing too hard for words to come out. The Rev helped her back to one of the wooden garden chairs that had been set up for dignitaries and the old. The mayor was seen with his arm around her, being a bit too comforting, Brenda would report later to Gary. Phineas Finn, a radio DJ from the local station, got up and played the acoustic guitar and a song he had written that very day for Stevie called "Buddy, We Luvs You, Come Home."

Gary had not gone to the vigil. Business was booming. The Ultramar picnic table, the dark alley behind the building, these were places Stevie had conducted his social and business interactions. He was part of the place. The Esso on the other end of town was probably wishing they hadn't given Stevie such a hard time for smoking near the pumps and sent him on his way. Gary heard people were boycotting the Esso for their treatment of Stevie, but he had only heard it from Brenda, and he knew the Esso had a bunch of *Missing* posters up in the store. When he drove past earlier, he saw the sign out front that usually advertised the price of gas and bananas now said *STevIE CoME HOME! ViEnna SauSAGE 2 4 1!* Either way, people were coming in to pick up a six-pack or carton of milk when they came to drop off a message for Stevie, or a drawing one of their children had made, encased in a zip-lock bag. And Gary's gas sales were up, a sign his perceived kindness towards Stevie was being rewarded.

Truth was, Gary couldn't stand the kid. He'd once caught his daughter walking down the street with him when she was only fourteen. Stevie was out of school by then, way too old for Kayla. It was just after he'd come back from his trip to the Pen. He was wheeling his bicycle along and Kayla was wearing one of those shirts that showed off her still childishly round belly, and pants that revealed one of the thongs Gary's ex-wife inexplicably let Kayla buy with her babysitting and birthday money. Kayla was laughing at something Stevie said. Gary made her get in the car and she refused to talk to him for three weeks. He bought her a new cell phone, as a bribe to resume communication, but he didn't tell her he'd put a tracker on it. The only reason he didn't chase Stevie off his property was if Stevie was sitting on the table outside the store, he knew he wasn't out lurking around his daughter. The last place Kayla would be caught was at her dad's gas station. Once Stevie was so high, he spent two hours walking around the Ultramar parking lot retracing the same figure-eight pattern. When Gary finally went out to talk to him, Stevie didn't hear him. Just kept walking like he was in a trance. Gary threatened to call the cops on Stevie more times than he could remember, but he never did. He knew by the time the cops actually showed up, Stevie would be long gone.

Stevie was a symptom of all that diseased this place, but he wasn't the cause, and the cops didn't have the time to chase him around unless he was actively engaging in armed robbery. They did come by when Stevie disappeared. Gary didn't tell them that they weren't the first to come looking for him, that days before, Carter had been in making inquiries, seeing if Stevie had been around that morning. Gary overheard this conversation from the backroom, but he didn't tell the cops about it, and Brenda didn't mention it either. Just acted all surprised. "Well, now you mention it, I haven't seen Stevie for a few days. Funny, I didn't notice." Gary saw one of the cops glance quickly towards her partner. But they didn't push their questions.

During the vigil, Gary set up the store's CCTV so it took in the growing memorial outside. Rumours that someone had stolen a pink teddy bear had caused tension amongst his part-time staff, so he had trained one of his cameras away from pump number two and onto the offerings that were piling up on the picnic table and hanging from the chain-link fence behind it.

Susie had gone to the vigil. She stood at the back, and one or two people gave her a nod of recognition, but mostly she was ignored. She felt uncomfortable, out of place, even though the event was at the little park she could see from her house. People gave her strange glances. Everyone else was with their people, and she didn't have people, not in the sense they meant it here. She half hoped one of the other Come-From-Aways might show up, and they could huddle on the edge of the crowd together.

Eight days earlier, about forty-five minutes into a run and Beyoncé ringing in her ears, Susie had loped along the trails and, in a kind of glee, leapt over puddles in the mud and breathed deep the forest smells. She was in the perfect loose-limbed, loose-minded state of moving forward with animal compulsion; of being a body running a brain, and not a brain running a body. She ran into the clearing, a place where kids partied. Both creepy and strangely beautiful as decades worth of broken glass littered the ground and caught the sun. It was a teenage sex-and-drugs kind of place. Her brain touched a memory of losing her virginity in a similar place in Ontario, less rock and more reeds, but just outside of town. She was considering this with the emotional detachment running afforded her, when her eyes saw it, red, attached to a leg. It took her endorphin-soaked animal brain a minute to catch up.

It was a shoe, a red, expensive-looking running shoe sticking out into the path ahead of her. She knew this shoe. It belonged to that kid, Stevie. The one she crossed the road to avoid. The one she was sure masturbated in the bushes. The chemical mix in her body was suddenly all wrong, adrenaline was pumping and she felt numb. She stopped running and her hearing went for a minute. She took out her earphones, but there was nothing, no wind or birdsong or distant highway sound. It happened before she fainted, this silence, but she couldn't faint, she needed to keep her shit together. Susie gasped for breath, her heart thumping from the sudden stop, her legs confused that they weren't still moving. The foot was still, and the leg was too. She could see an ATV pulled up just beside the trail.

Susie wanted him to be asleep. She was scared of this kid, despite his scrawny arms and underdog appearance, he always reminded her of a really hungry and unpredictable animal. She pitied him, but she didn't trust him. She had stopped running the trails for a while because of him, then when she had stopped seeing him around town, she had started heading up through the woods again. Something in the way he used to nod his head at her made her feel naked. But his head wasn't nodding now. She let her eyes travel up to his face and for a moment she thought it was a trap, and he was going to grab her.

His eyes were wide open. Ants were crawling all over his cheeks, a line travelling over his lips. It was the ants that tipped her from cautious concern to fear and she bolted, getting away as far as she could. She ran right past the police station, and kept going far out towards the lake until her legs were like jelly and she turned slowly and took a plodding jog back towards her house.

She had to call the police, but then she imagined the conversation, and them asking, "Why didn't you call straight away?" To be honest, she wasn't sure. She'd pressed the nine then the one, then she stopped. The telephone always made her hyperventilate. She'd heard that therapist on the radio say you should make notes if you have phone anxiety. She did it when she had to call the vet's, or the doctor's, or order pizza; appointment for Sam, pap smear, anchovies. Her head was pounding.

She went upstairs and found some pills, swallowed three, got in the shower.

She realized she had to go back. Go back and calmly reassess the situation. She would take Sam this time. She would touch the boy, maybe prod him with a stick to make sure, before she called the cops.

She drank a whisky to calm her nerves, and then another. Day drinking was an exception, not the rule, but she was drinking like a possessed woman. Bad drinking. Not the sip, sip kind but the drowning kind, the kind to make everything go away. She pretended to herself the drinking was working until she was seasick, crawling to the toilet then puking, puking, puking. It was early evening when she woke up on the bathroom floor, Sam licking her hair. Shakes, self-recriminations. She fed the dog and went to bed. She would go back tomorrow. She would call the police from the body. She would apologize to the kid. She would confess to the police, lie just a little. Say she hadn't gotten close, had found him scary, figured he was sleeping, but then she started to worry and went back to check the next day.

It was early, 6 a.m., the following morning. She'd already showered off the sweat and tears and booze of the day before. Her stomach held her guilt like a nest of snakes. She put Sam on his lead, and they headed up to the clearing. Susie took the direct route, no fucking around. They never went out this early. Susie was not one of those morning people, the soft light, the emptiness, the air seeming new, it just irritated her. She would have to touch. Feel with her hand the cold flesh. She hoped things hadn't eaten him. She had a horrible vision of maggots writhing in his eyes.

They got there fast, the dog excited to be out so early. As they got closer, Sam was not tugging on the leash, he was just moseying ahead of her, like nothing was up. She didn't see the shoes, the kid must be further along than she remembered, but she walked the length of the trail where it cut through the clearing, and nothing. No dead boy. No ATV. Nothing.

The feel of it, the relief, when it lifted from her shoulders. She was high with redemption. She had nothing to confess. She was guilty and not guilty. Guilty of not checking, but there was nothing wrong after all. But then she thought of the ants. The ants crawling on his face, and the white pallor of his skin. She contemplated calling the cops still, but saying what? "There is nothing here, and for reasons I can hardly explain I got drunk instead of reporting what I found to you yesterday. I don't deal well with life, with human contact" sounds pretty trite in an I-found-a-body situation.

But he was gone, and maybe it was some kind of hoax? A trick? Or maybe she'd just imagined the whole thing; the trees, the physical exertion, the quantity of time she spent alone since Evelyn had left for what was initially a work sabbatical, but turned out to be a relationship one too, finally tipping Susie into psychosis? An unease followed her for the next week, and then she heard the news report: Stevie Loder, of Bay Mal Verde, was missing.

~

Kev had gone to the vigil with his mom. People were pretending to have hope of Stevie's safe return then. "Sin," she'd said when they got there, and again when Hugh Dooley showed up drunk, and again when Arlene got up then couldn't stop crying enough to speak. He'd seen Evie there with Brenda, tried to catch her eye, but she was staring at the ground most of the time.

Kev was relieved when they found Stevie's ATV at the bottom of the cliff. He didn't think anyone would find Stevie, but you never knew. The woods held a lot of secrets, and you never knew when it was going to give one of them up. A hunter found a grenade once. He went for a piss and saw something in the undergrowth. Him and his buddies carried it around for two days and when he got home his wife made him take it to the cop shop. They said it could have gone off at any moment. Had experts come in and explode the thing in an empty field. It was from the Second World War, and they figured a soldier had brought it home, thought better of it, and dumped it out there. The woods were fickle. Kev's uncle had dropped a Swiss Army knife once and it had just disappeared, he'd made Kev crawl around for an hour and he never found it. Three weeks later they were back in the same spot and there it was, easy to see, almost lying on top of a rock, red plastic case so obvious amongst muted browns and greens. Surely they'd have spotted it if it had been there when they first lost it.

Once they found the ATV, at the bottom of a cliff and half-submerged in the ocean, the ground searches for Stevie stopped. They sent down divers, but the conditions were poor and they didn't find anything. There was talk of trying to raise enough money to bring in that couple with the underwater drone, but the currents were so strong, and the seas so rough, that no one really expected Stevie's body to be found. Arlene said she knew, she'd felt it for days, that her child was dead. And although no one said it, Stevie was the kind of guy you expected to die young and tragic.

Kev thought about joining one of the searches, but decided that was too much. On the cop shows on TV, the murderer always showed up to look for the body, and he wasn't going to make that mistake. And then, after the ATV was found, when someone started a campaign to buy a headstone for Stevie, somewhere for Arlene to go and make her peace with this world and Stevie's death, Kev saw an opportunity for a kind of atonement.

Stevie disappeared in the fall, and in the spring the tombstone was erected. An oval picture of Stevie taken a few years earlier, wearing his IceCaps jacket and the D&G ball cap he was so proud of but lost at a party a week after he got it, was stuck on a slab of granite. Stevie was smiling in the picture, giving the camera a two-fingered salute. Above the photograph were the words *In Loving Memory* and below it his name, *Steven Aloysius Loder*. Under Stevie's name was an etching of an ATV, but it must have been a generic one because the machine pictured on the tombstone was a way better one than Stevie had ever owned. "Maybe he's got a real sweet ride in heaven," Carter said that night when they ended up at the cemetery drunk and pouring whisky on the place where Stevie's body should have been.

~

Susie waited a few weeks before she went to pay her respects to Stevie. She wanted to bring flowers but all they had at the Food Basics in Carbonear was marked fifty per cent off. Sad carnations, Gerbera daisies dyed electric blue and pink with some limp-stemmed and brown-leafed fern thrown in. The stems of the daisies encased in plastic tubes. She didn't buy them.

She was relieved to be alone, not to run into Arlene or the groupie mourners, as she had come to think of them. A group of junior-high girls had taken to hanging around the Ultramar, Stevie's old haunt, playing sad songs from their telephones, eating candy, vaping and occasionally sticking a fake flower or strange stuffed animal on a keychain into the chain-link fence behind the store. It was unclear if any of them knew Stevie. They were a generation younger than him. Susie had seen them up at the cemetery from a distance when she was out with Sam. They were dancing around Stevie's grave in a combination of worship and degradation. Susie remembered her own teenage obsession with Jim Morrison, there was something very seductive about a heartbreaking, but safe, crush on a dead boy. As she stood by the marble slab, the dog lifted his leg against the corner of the stone before Susie could stop him. "Sorry," she said. "I'm so sorry."

The first time it happened, Susie was running the trail, and she swore Stevie was standing in the woods just to her left, his hands down his pants. *Can ghosts masturbate?* the pragmatic part of her wondered. It was a hallucination, she decided, brought on by stress. But Stevie popped up in other places. A quick flash on his bicycle on her way to the post office. Once peering in the kitchen window, which made her scream. Sitting on the curb smoking a cigarette. Sprawled on her sofa, looking up at her. It was always just a flash. A few seconds. He was stroking Sam, crouched down in the backyard, the dog sitting looking up at him. One of the cats refused to sit on her previously favourite chair, and another hissed periodically at the empty seat at the kitchen table. Susie bought a sage stick online and tried to smudge the house, but it just made her eyes water and Sam insisted on going into the backyard and wouldn't come in for a long time. The thing smelled vaguely chemical.

~

Susie was waiting in line at the Ultramar. Gary noticed her come in, he hadn't seen her much all winter or spring, but a warm June day was bringing everyone out. Susie was looking older, she'd lost weight, but not in a good way and her hair was dull. He'd heard her "friend" was living on the mainland. Gary was always slower than the women that worked for him, and customers fidgeted in line anxious to make their purchases. Susie was trying not to stare at the guy in front of her, everyone was giving him a wide berth, the tattoos on his face like magical markings parting the crowds in his way. But he nodded and smiled at everyone coming in the door and they nodded back cautiously. One of them even said, "How's you doing, Kev?"

"Grand, b'y. Just grand."

It was just after that when Susie saw Stevie again. Pale, like in real life, but shoeless. He was always shoeless when she saw him, wearing white tube socks that dripped with mud. He was leaning up against the slushy machines, sipping from a super-sized cup. Blue slush and red layered in the cup. She stared, she wanted to catch the moment he disappeared. But something pulled her attention away. The guy in front of her was motionless, not stepping forward to take his place in front of the till, he was looking over towards where she'd seen Stevie, his face completely still, until his eyebrow twitched. He must have felt her looking at him because he turned and their eyes locked, then they both glanced back towards the slushy machines, but Stevie was gone. A melting cup of slush sat next to the machine, and neither of them could be sure if it was there before.

THAT RUNNING GIRL

~

I see her all the time, running by the house. They call it running these days, but she's just jogging. And she's not that fast. I don't know what the fuck's wrong with her, always coming up here sweating and red faced. We're at the top of the hill and by the time she gets here she's always beat out. I keep worrying she's going to have a goddamn heart attack outside the house and I'll be the one that has to deal with it. Every couple of days she comes running up the street. I watch her struggling up it, and then she heads down the ATV trail. Few people walk up to where we're at; it's too damn steep.

I get enough exercise keeping the house clean. From what I hear, that running girl doesn't spend much time cleaning. My sister Regina lives across the road from that maid and her *friend*. She's never been over since they bought the place. But her grandkids have. They were collecting for Shave for the Brave (Tyra should never have gone through with it, she looked some shocking with no hair) and they went into them girls' house asking for a donation. Evie said the place stank like cat piss and there was hair everywhere. Big dustballs of it. They don't even let the poor things outside, according to Regina. And their dog went crazy barking at the kids when they knocked on the door. She gave them some money though.

At least today the girl's got clothes on. Sometimes she comes by here with most of her bra showing. My husband will be out there tinkering with the mower and will yell out, "Yer speeding!" or some crap and she'll wave and smile, boobs flopping all around as she goes past the house. Practically gives him a hard-on.

She goes out in all weather. Doesn't matter if it's raining or snowing or if there's a wicked wind. And what the fuck's she running from anyways? Not like she's trying to catch a man. The only people who run around here are the ones that work in town, and a couple of the teachers. Most of us never have time for it.

Maybe the other one likes her to keep skinny. For a while Regina thought they were just friends or sisters or something, but then her son, Sean Jr., said he seen them making out. "Tongues and everything. Just like a porno right out in the open," he said. And Regina said she seen them kiss too. Although, she didn't think they were frenching.

When the house sold, we all figured maybe someone bought it for the summer. You see that here sometimes, some rich couple comes gallivanting round the bay on the one hot day of the summer, and imagine it's like that here all the time. They'll show up the next year from Texas or Toronto and will act all surprised when it's August and only seven degrees. When that finger of fog comes poking down the harbour and the cold air hits, you can practically hear the *For Sale* signs going back up. Not them girls, they moved in straight away and stayed all winter. Regina thought they might be growing drugs. They had all these plants and lights in the window. Sean Jr. did some plumbing work for them. Turns out it was just tomato plants.

They say she's some kind of artist. But no one's ever seen what she does.

What the hell does she do all day in that big house? Regina says no one ever visits her. I'd get lonely. There's always someone dropping by here. I think I seen that girl talking to herself when she's going by. Not surprising, amount of time she spends alone.

I seen Stevie Loder talking to her the other day. Didn't like the way he was looking at her. She smiled and said something to him but you could tell that smile was fake. She kept on going even when he yelled at her to stop a minute. She pretended like she couldn't hear him but I think she could. I seen him mouth "Bitch" at her back after she ran past him.

Stevie was always a small kid. He was in the same grade as Regina's grandson Carter, but was always only half Carter's size. When Barb was in nursing school, she used to tell us that's what happened when you smoked when you were pregnant, the baby would come out all small and runt-like, like Stevie. When Tyra's mom, Lisa-Marie, was pregnant, Barb was always giving Lisa-Marie a hard time about the dangers of cigarettes and using little Stevie as an example.

I knew the Loders a bit. Stevie's dad, Harold Loder, always had a reputation for being a hard ticket. Harold's sister married real young, and everyone said it was to get away from him. He was in his thirties when he married Arlene, and she was only twenty-two. It wasn't unknown for Arlene to be walking around with a black eye or bruised cheek, she'd be saying the same old line about being real clumsy. We all know it's pretty hard to be clumsy with your own face. Things got easier for her when Harold died. "Industrial accident" they said at the time, but how he came to drive off the dock "accidentally" is still something people talk about. Some say it was some of the b'ys from the plant getting him back for when Clarence Snow lost his leg. Harold was driving the forklift when that frozen cod slipped off the pallet and smashed right down on Clarence. He had to stop working, I seen him at the mall in his wheelchair, with one leg of his pants cut short and pinned together with a clothes peg.

Maybe guilt drove Harold to it. He did some bad things to Arlene. There were rumours Harold did worse things to Cheryl. She got sent off to live with an aunt in Corner Brook. Never comes to see her mother. Maybe blames her for whatever Harold got up to.

Not many people were sad to see Harold gone. I still went to the visitation though. Arlene looked like a ghost and Cheryl didn't show up, even for the funeral. I made my husband come with me. "Why we got to go to that?" he said to me. "You don't care about Arlene, you just want to see who shows up." But he was wrong, it's important to show your respect to the relatives, even if the dead was a damn bastard.

Stevie, he dropped out of school as soon as he could. He never really grew up, just stayed small and lean. The local girls all know to stay away from him. There are stories of him taking advantage of some girl passed out at a party and I saw him hanging out at the park a few times, talking to girls too young for him to be talking to. Made sure he knew I was there watching and he went on his way. He's never been charged for it. And girls do lie about these things. I don't know. There is something about him, something about the way he looks at women that doesn't feel right.

And the drugs of course. The drugs don't help matters. Regina's seen what they done to Tyra's mother. Says she can't hardly recognize her when she's high. Then there was the stealing. Regina couldn't leave anything out if Lisa-Marie was coming to visit. When she needed a fix, she was dangerous. Left Tyra alone for hours when she was a baby and she was out trying to make money. Regina and her husband got custody in the end. Sean Jr. was practically a child himself when Tyra was born.

And Regina's grandson Carter, the drugs got him in trouble, she says that's all over, that he's reformed, but I know the company that boy keeps.

Stevie's had a real dangerous look recently. He sometimes says hello to me. "Hello, Mrs. Molloy, some grand day we're having." He says it in a way that sounds like it should be friendly but it's not. Whenever he talks to me, I feel like it's some kind of threat. Never even looks my way if my husband is around. Only talks to me when I'm alone.

There's Stevie now, out there on some bike. Looks like he stole it from a sixth grader. Probably did. He's weaving back and forth across the road like some kind of snake. Who's he waiting for? If it's Carter, I'll have to tell Regina.

Stevie's down the bottom of the hill now. Looks like he's thinking of coming back but he can't bike up. He tried but it's too steep and so he's given up. He just looked round to see if anyone's seen him make a fool of himself. He can't see me. The blinds are down. Thank God for that.

~

I'm up early looking out the window, and I see Stevie lurking up at the trail. I thought he was a moose at first when I seen a dark shape in the trees. I think he must be having a piss, or worse, but he's been there too long now and it doesn't feel right. I see his bike now, shoved up in the woods. Who's he waiting for?

Jesus. Now I see her, that running girl coming up the hill heading straight towards him. I just caught a glimpse of Stevie's face. Eyes cold and he's not smiling. I'm out the door before I think about it.

"Hey," I bawl out at her soon as I'm outside. "Hey, maid, come here a minute!" She looks at me and looks confused. But she slows down, takes out her earbuds.

"Are you okay?" she says like she's expecting me to have a finger cut off or my husband to be lying on the ground somewhere and I need her to give him mouth-to-mouth. I look up towards the trail at Stevie and she follows my gaze. I see her notice the lurid-pink bicycle poking out through the long grass and Stevie crouched down in the background.

"You live by my sister, Regina." I'm not so good with small talk and I don't know what to say about Stevie.

"I do, right across the road." We both stare up at Stevie as we talk. She understands what I'm telling her. Stevie must have seen we've both been watching him and stands up. That girl's gone pretty pale and she makes some stupid comment about the weather as we both watch Stevie come out of the undergrowth get on his bike and weave down the street towards us. He doesn't stop or speak, just stares at us and then, right in front of where we're standing, he rides in a circle on the street. Makes a point of going slow and just manages to make it round without falling over. Normally, I would have laughed at him. Me and that girl, neither of us say nothing, we just watch Stevie. He looks out of it today. Really fucked up. He circles once then coasts down the hill and out of our sight.

"He's not right, maid," I say and when I look at her, I see she has her hands clasped behind her back to stop them from shaking.

"Thanks," she says. "Thank you."

"You tell Regina to give me a call." There's no need for us to talk more about Stevie. And she nods and starts jogging very slowly up the hill. She doesn't take the trail like usual though, but turns up to the lake road.

~

I seen that girl running again today. We waved to each other when she ran by and she called out, "Nice day, Bernie."

My husband was a bit miffed because it was me she was looking for and not him. "Maybe she's got a crush on you," he said all smirking. And I told him to fuck right off and what if she do? That surprised him.

BOYS

~

They rolled around the neighbourhood together, a clump of boy. They would shed a boy at one house and pick a new one up at the next corner. They gave off a smell of Vienna sausage, farts and fabric softener. You could hear them coming, sometimes from the sound of running feet, or of bike tires screeching, but most often from laughter and shouts. They buzzed with energy. They were always moving. It was just before the time of puberty that would make them want to sleep and lie about in dark bedrooms. They were at an age when they wanted to leap and run and climb.

They had pink lips, rosy cheeks and foul mouths. When they were out on the streets together, swear words punctuated their speech in a staccato rhythm.

Kev, Justin, Carter, Ryan, and Stevie. They had just finished grade six, except for Justin who was a year ahead. Justin and Kev were the same age, but Kev had been held back the year his sister died and he missed so much school. He and Justin were the tallest. Kev was thick and Justin was lean. Carter was a foot shorter than Kev, but that wouldn't last for long. Ryan was around the same height as Carter but his shoulders were still kid-like, sloping down, his edges still curved where Carter's had started to square. Stevie was that kid in the class who stayed a head shorter than everyone else and was always at the front in the school photo. He was always with the other boys, but never invited. He followed them around, an eager and often abused groupie, like an annoying younger sibling or a sucker fish attaching itself to a shark.

It was the first Saturday since school had let out for the summer. Ryan was helping his dad pack up the camper van. It was just after lunch, and they were leaving first thing the next morning. His parents would wake him early, and Ryan would climb into his seat still in his pajamas. Ryan's mom was inside cleaning, and Ryan and his dad had been sent out of her way so she could perform a ritualized house-leaving, making sure everything was in place for their return. Both of his parents were in their pre-vacation bad mood, arguing about the route they should take, and whether they should stop for lunch or have sandwiches in the van to save time. None of it would matter once they got moving. His dad would turn up the radio and his mom would put her feet up on the dashboard.

Ryan felt the buzz of the other boys coming before he saw them. He sensed them, his pack arriving, like a wave of static electricity over the fine blond hairs on his arms. They were zipping back and forth across the road. Dashing in different directions then coming together. When they saw Ryan's dad, they assimilated into a group and slowed their pace. They came sedately, Kev out front as their spokesperson, the other boys hanging back, a little giggly, because parents were funny, even though they all had them.

"You want a hand, Mr. Cole?" Kev asked.

"No. We're almost done here," Ryan's dad said.

The boys fidgeted behind Kev. Ryan's dad looked at Ryan and he gestured his head, a quick upwards tilt, and Ryan was released.

Ryan and the other boys walked until they were out of sight and earshot of his dad, then they took off running and Justin yelled, "Fuck!" for no particular reason.

They dipped and darted, shoving each other back and forth. Justin pushed Stevie out into the street when a car was coming down towards them. The car had not been going fast, and the driver braked then laid on the horn. Justin gave the car the finger and they all ran like the driver was chasing them. They headed up to the schoolyard, slowing their pace and, by now, more subdued and scuffing at the ground with their running shoes as they walked.

At the school, they headed around back to a patch of concrete. They weren't allowed here during recess. It was out of sight of the road and classroom windows. The place Big Bill the janitor smoked illicit cigarettes next to the same blue metal dumpster the grade eight kids were rumoured to commit rudimentary sex acts behind. Finger Fuck Alley, the kids called the space between the dumpster and the wall of the school. On weekdays, when the teachers' parking lot emptied, and on the weekends when the school was deserted, the boys took over this space. They could be their unconscious selves here, without anyone reporting back to their mothers. They didn't have to guard their expressions, or obscure their intentions, it was a place where they made their own rules.

They set up their game wordlessly. Two chunks of black asphalt that the snow plough had scraped up during the winter made up the goalposts. Kev fished a balding yellow tennis ball from his jacket pocket. Carter started out as goalie; he always did and no one knew why, least of all Carter. They had been playing this game together since kindergarten. No one ever won and it didn't have a name, although Ryan thought of it sometimes as "Ball" and Stevie thought of it as "Kick."

Ryan scored first (he usually did) and replaced Carter in goal. He had the best footwork of all of them. Justin and Kev both concentrated on taking the ball by a combination of intimidation and brute force. Ryan got good at keeping the ball away from them by darting around them and kicking the ball through gaps in their moving legs. Carter could make the ball move where he wanted it to, he had excellent aim, but when the game got slow, jammed up by Justin and Kev bullying the ball off each other, he wanted to prove he was as tough as they were, and began muscling in on the action, forgetting the purpose of the game was scoring not shoving. Stevie, when he got the ball, tended to make rash shots, sending the ball flying past the two goal markers and bouncing away from them through the parking lot. The other boys would wait as he ran after it, heckling him to hurry the fuck up and mumbling to each other that he ran like a girl.

Justin scored, then Kev, then Ryan again. Stevie made one of his wild kicks, the ball was in the air up over Ryan's head then it bounced once, but it must have hit a stone, or some peculiar fault in the paving, because it rose almost straight up in the air, then veered left and landed with an audible thud in the dark-blue metal dumpster beside the school. They heard the ball bounce around a few times, then it stopped.

"Fucking retard," Justin said.

The dumpster was usually full of garbage. The boys often boosted Stevie up over its edge. Their ball would be sitting on top of a pile of plump black garbage bags, bits of old desks and chairs. Stevie would toss the ball out then jump down following it.

Kev, Carter, and Stevie went to the dumpster. The two bigger boys lifted Stevie up until he could reach the lip of the dumpster, then he grabbed onto it and hauled himself up and over. The boys watched his two hands clutching at the other side of the dumpster's rim, then disappearing as he let go. They heard Stevie's feet hitting the bottom, a sound like a cat jumping from a table to the floor.

The ball came flying out and Carter caught it, dropped it to his feet, and the game commenced immediately. Carter scored. He was celebrating, pumping his fist saying, "Who's the fucking champion!" when they heard Stevie calling out to them.

"Hey! Hey!" he was yelling, trying to get their attention.

They all looked towards the dumpster.

"Stevie?" Kev called.

"I'm fucking stuck."

The boys started laughing. Only Kev's voice had started to break and his laughter had a weird crackling quality. The other boys' laughter was high pitched and out of control. Together they sounded like a bunch of hyenas.

Stevie was making a sound too, a noise in between laughing and crying.

They were recovering themselves, were straightening up and wiping their eyes, they were preparing to begrudgingly rescue Stevie who was crying and calling out. Begging and swearing at them.

"Help me, b'ys, please. You motherfuckers! Get me out

of here, you assholes! Fucking assholes! Please, please, get me out. Ryan, you there? Help me, buddy."

They were approaching the dumpster, taking their time, listening to the emotion building in Stevie's voice. It had little effect on them, they were used to seeing Stevie cry, his face scrunched and red in frustration.

"Use your words, Stevie," Carter joked, something one of their teachers used to say to him.

It was in reaction to Carter's teasing that Stevie threw the orange out of the dumpster at them. It was an underhand lob, but none of them were expecting it, and it landed, like a particularly large shit from a seagull, directly on top of Justin's head. It was a soft, fermenting piece of fruit, rotted on one side, it perched like an exotic bird on the nest of Justin's hair before rolling off and down his back leaving a viscous liquid, a citrusy snot, behind.

"Fuck, fuck, fuck, fuck." Justin shook his head around. Then he stopped and was silent. A dangerous silence. He stood still and the other boys watched, waiting to see what he did next. Kev cocked his head to one side. Carter's mouth twitched from a grin to a scowl trying out different emotions. Ryan counted backwards from ten in his head and made it to three.

"I'm gonna kill you, Stevie," Justin said, his voice low and slow.

Justin grabbed the orange from the ground, pulp dripped from his clenched fist. He threw it towards the dumpster. It was too decomposed and damaged to hold together and it fell apart as it left his hand. Gobs of sticky orange flesh, like bits of roadkill, spattered in front of him. He picked up the tennis ball and hurled it at the dumpster, the ball rolled back to him and he kicked it again and again making the dumpster's metal side echo thunderously.

Stevie was eerily silent.

The ball bounced off the dumpster and Justin missed it. It rolled away from them. Carter ran to retrieve it and they could hear Stevie again.

"Fuck, b'ys, get me outta here. It's not fucking funny."

"It's not fucking funny," Justin mimicked him. Then he picked up a rock, it wasn't big, but it was the kind that could hurt and definitely damage an eye, he tossed it from hand to hand, and then he whipped it at the side of the dumpster.

Justin scanned the ground for more ammunition. His eyes flickered across the asphalt goalposts. He picked one up, it was heavy, a different proposition than the small rock. Kev, Carter, and Ryan watched Justin throw it carefully and languidly up in the air then held their breath as it came down fast and heavy into the dumpster, where Stevie was stuck. Stevie screamed. But they had heard the metal clunk that meant he hadn't been hit with Justin's projectile.

"Let me out, let me out," Stevie was yelling.

Justin picked up the other goalpost, a look of malicious intent in his eye. He was no longer playing. Carter was laughing a nervous giggle, throwing the tennis ball from hand to hand. Ryan was counting just under his breath, "Three, two, one...ten, nine," then Kev spoke up. "This is shit. I'm fucking bored," and he started to walk away from Stevie, from the dumpster, from being an audience for Justin.

Justin looked at Carter and Ryan, but neither of them met his eye. He lobbed the hunk of asphalt at the side of the dumpster and then he followed after Kev, and Carter joined him. Ryan hesitated.

"Hello?" Stevie called out. "Is anyone there?"

Ryan walked towards the dumpster. Justin turned around and yelled at him, "Don't be a faggot, Ryan. Just leave the fucking crybaby. Come on." Ryan looked towards the others and saw orange pulp stuck in the back of Justin's hair.

Ryan stood still and watched as the others walked away. When they rounded the corner of the school and were out of view he went back to the dumpster. Ryan looked around, there was a broken pallet leaning against the back door of the school. He dragged it over, getting splinters in his hand, and leaned it against the dumpster. He used the pallet like a ladder, and climbed up it, he rested his elbows on the edge of the dumpster and looked in. It stank, the smell reminded Ryan of the pit toilets at campsites and the mouldy lunch he had pulled out of the back of his desk at the end of the school year. Stevie was standing in the back corner, staring up at him snot nosed and teary eyed.

"I'm not fucking crying," he said.

The dumpster was deep and completely empty, except for the hunk of paving Justin had flung in, and a wet-looking clump in one corner that seemed like it might be some kind of rancid meat and cloth. Ryan decided not to look in that corner again. Stevie came over and reached up to Ryan. He grabbed Ryan's hand. Stevie's hand was warm and sticky. Ryan wasn't strong enough to pull him up. He was afraid to lean any further over in case Stevie managed to grab him and haul him right over and into the dumpster. If one of the other boys was around, they could have worked together to lift the pallet up and into the dumpster so Stevie could use it. Ryan tried, but he could not lift it high enough. Ryan considered getting in the dumpster with Stevie and then giving him a boost out, but then Ryan would be stuck, dependent on Stevie to free him.

"I'm gonna get help," Ryan said.

"Fuck, no. We'll get in trouble." Stevie was pacing now, back and forth, back and forth, in the small space. His veins seemed to glow blue underneath his pale white skin. Ryan didn't want to be there, watching. Stevie had started to punch the side of the dumpster at regular intervals. He had ripped off part of a fingernail with his teeth and his finger was bleeding.

"I'll get my dad. He won't be mad," Ryan said. He knew his dad would not be mad at Stevie. He wouldn't be mad at Ryan either, worse, he would be disappointed. He knew the look his dad would give him, the quiet shake of his head, how he wouldn't tell his mom, but wouldn't look Ryan in the eye for a few weeks. "Disappointed. Expected better of you." Ryan would prefer a quick flash of anger than the slow burn of shame.

"Don't fucking leave me!" Stevie screamed.

Ryan talked to him softly. "It'll be okay, Stevie. I'll run home, grab my dad—"

"No! Don't fucking leave me!"

"Okay, okay."

Ryan wasn't allowed to go into Stevie or Justin's houses. The boys rarely hung out inside, although sometimes they had been to Carter's to watch TV, and sometimes to Kev's where his mom always had Pepsi. Ryan never invited the boys over. He didn't want them to see the teddy bear on his bed, and he knew his mom didn't really approve of the other boys, although she never exactly said so. When she went to the store and Carter's mom was working, she called her Brenda, but Carter's mom called Ryan's mom Mrs. Cole. He didn't think once about getting Stevie's mom, Arlene, and Stevie didn't suggest it either.

~

Ryan was sitting outside of the dumpster, his back leaning against it. Stevie was on the other side, his back mirroring Ryan's. Every few minutes, Stevie would say, "You still there, Ryan?" and Ryan would say, "Yep." He was trying to decide what he should do, when he heard whistling.

He looked up and saw Kev headed towards him with a ladder balanced on his shoulder.

Kev propped the ladder up on the edge of the dumpster, and Ryan climbed back up the pallet and helped guide it in. It was aluminum, light and easy to maneuver. Stevie grabbed the ladder from its bottom legs. He leaned it against the side of the dumpster and was up and out of it like a silverfish. He didn't stop to say anything once he was free, he just took off running away from Ryan and Kev and disappeared between the trees at the edge of the schoolyard.

Ryan reached in to grab the ladder.

"Just leave it," Kev said.

"Where'd you get it?" Ryan asked.

Kev shook his head and took off whistling.

The next morning Ryan and his parents left at 6 a.m. and as they drove down the street, Ryan caught a glimpse of Stevie already out, pedalling around on a pink bicycle.

~

Three days until Christmas, his exams behind him. Gifts from downtown stores wrapped up under his bed for his mom, dad and nan, Ryan was filled with joy. He felt right. Everything about his life was good. He loved his dorm room, his classes, waiting in line each morning to order his Americano with one sugar (the raw brown crumbly kind if it was available). His last day of classes, Terresa

Barnes had sat beside him in class and handed him her phone. Ryan had entered his number. He had only been gone since September, but he had changed; no longer the teenager who wore the clothes his mom picked out for him at Mark's Work Wearhouse. He was a man (though still technically in his teens) who bought his own pants, with rips in them, from Value Village and the Salvation Army. He only wore black T-shirts now, and he had an old work jacket from the Come By Chance oil refinery, navy with the name *Stan* on the arm. The jacket was not warm enough for the winter, so he wore it with a black wool cable-knit sweater.

It was snowing delicate flakes. Ryan's parents had a real tree, already decorated. His aunt was over and he had sat around the table with her and his mom and dad having a few drinks. His mom pink faced after an unusual third glass of Riunite. Ryan had a nice little pre-buzz before he headed out. The bar was just minutes from the house. Half the time it was empty, the only part of it regularly occupied were the seats at the VLT machines, the same weathered faces sitting on familiar stools, feeding their hopes and dreams into the machines' payment slots. Tonight one of the local cover bands was playing and it seemed like everyone Ryan had gone to high school with was out. The bar was loud already, the band playing "Dirty Old Town" when he arrived and Ryan felt like he was walking onto a movie set of the biopic of his own life. His crowd from high school was sitting at a table, they all called out "Ryan" in chorus as he approached.

He couldn't pinpoint when his feeling of sentimental bliss was replaced by a kernel of dissatisfaction. Perhaps when Krista Mercer started complaining about how shitty downtown St. John's was, or how she didn't understand her math prof, how he hardly spoke English and then imitated him speaking. Chad Butt was telling him how awesome his new PlayStation was, and Ryan felt himself apart. They were the same, they had gone away, but returned unchanged. He was disappointed. He thought they would talk about important things, not about the same mundane shit that they had all through high school: TV, celebrities, their pregnant classmates. It was like none of them had changed at all. He went for a smoke.

"When did he start smoking?" Krista Mercer's voice echoed after him. "And what's the point of an English degree? You can't get a job with that."

Ryan stood outside. The Christmas lights across the road on the town's tree sparkling. He heard his childhood companions first, before he saw them.

"That fucking bitch. Thinks she goddamn owns me 'cause she sucked me off when I was drunk. Wants to know what I'm getting her for Christmas, so I sent her a picture of my dick." Justin. He and Carter, back from the oil fields, were getting out of a truck. They both had thick arms and shiny eyes. When they walked towards him, Ryan turned away from the door, hoping they wouldn't notice him, but he was too late. They were there beside him, feeling sociable. They wanted to tell him about the size of their paycheques. They couldn't believe he was paying to read books, when he could be out where the action was. Justin all buddy this, buddy that, and they pulled him back into the bar with them. He saw his high-school friends watch his return, Krista Mercer gave him an appraising look but Ryan didn't disentangle himself from Justin and Carter, he let himself be pulled along and settled between them, leaning up at the bar. They started buying him drinks. Ryan had a little money, but before he could open his wallet to pay for a round, the Fort Mac cash was on the table. Ryan was drinking beer, and so was Justin. Carter drank top-shelf whisky in watered-down fountain Pepsi.

Justin started to speak of hitting that pussy. Ryan saw these words and imagined Justin's child self mouthing them. He imagined the pink-lipped, chapped-cheeked kids he used to play with. Remembered Carter in a scarf his nan had knit and Justin always in a Maple Leafs toque, sent from Ontario by his absent father.

At 1 a.m., the table of his high-school friends got up to go. Andrew Butt came by. "We're headed to Krista's. Karaoke? You wanna come?"

"You inviting all of us?" Justin cackled. "I loves a bit of karaoke. What's your favourite song now b'y, 'Dancing Queen'?"

"Naaah, I'm good," said Ryan. His words were stretched and slow.

"You sure?" Andrew asked. Ryan knew he was loaded. He could hear his own voice slurring.

"Yes, he's fucking sure," Justin said. Andrew shrugged and walked away.

"Fucking faggot," Carter mumbled, but Andrew just let the words slide off his back.

They were outside smoking a joint when Stevie Loder came along the street towards them. He was still scrawny. He had a thin moustache on his upper lip that was slightly shorter on the left-hand side. It looked almost as though it had been drawn on with marker, and Ryan was tempted to reach out and try and rub it off. For a moment felt his hand hovering towards Stevie before he quickly withdrew it, and he understood in that moment he should go home.

"You go on, b'ys. I think I might call it a night." Ryan spoke each word carefully, concentrating on them individually to make sure they sounded right.

"No way, my son. You're out with us tonight. We're going hard," Justin said.

The stuff they smoked outside the bar was different from what he was used to. Ryan was pretty sure it was the kind of pot that could give you psychosis. Again, Ryan said, "I think I should just go home now."

"Don't be such a faggot," Justin said.

"Yeah, don't be a fag," Stevie giggled.

Ryan didn't remember crossing the street to get to it, but he was at Justin's truck and Carter was opening the door and Ryan found himself climbing in the back seat. Justin laughed when Ryan missed on his first attempt to climb into the high cab and stumbled back. When he got in, everything was spinning, then Stevie scrambled up and into the seat beside him. Justin was driving fast, fast. He and Carter lit another joint and were passing it back and forth. A glowing ember kept coming close to his face. Stevie was trying to hand Ryan the joint and laughing at him.

"He's gone, b'ys. He's fucking gone."

"I'm going to puke," Ryan said. The third time Justin heard him and he pulled off the road. "Don't fucking hurl in my ride."

Justin's truck pulled up in front of the church and the four of them stumbled out, Ryan taking in deep breaths. He was nauseous and at the same time experiencing a chemically induced belief in his own indestructibility. His eyes were wide open, he couldn't close or relax them. He was not sure if he was hallucinating.

The Catholic church was huge, a towering thing built for the grand town that Bay Mal Verde was supposed to be. The merchants Ryan was descended from had a tendency toward excess and bankruptcy. Bay Mal Verde was left with a basilica it could not really afford. Its towers had recently been reinforced with concrete and the building wore a permanent dress of scaffolding. The grounds were large and mostly dark. There was a larger than life-sized nativity scene set up and lit with a spotlight to the left side of it. Mary and Joseph huddled under a shelter made of roughly cut logs with a roof of branches cut from pine trees. They gazed down at the iridescent porcelain head of their newborn son. They loomed larger than they should have over the plaster sheep and donkey they shared the stable with. The three wise men and one shepherd were a slightly smaller scale. They were placed just outside of the shelter, facing the main street like they were having a smoke outside of a nightclub. The church faced the ocean and no buildings were in front of it, only Water Street, deserted at this time of night.

"I gotta piss," said Carter. He headed towards the imposing building and the others followed. They stopped when they got to the church's stone steps, and Carter walked away from them, behind a tree and they all listened to the stream of his urine being released.

"That's a fucking relief," he said as he returned to them. A truck came down the street blaring "The Mummer's Song." A drunk Santa stood in the flatbed of the truck, a beer in his hand, yelling out, "Merry Christmas, ho ho ho!"

"Merry Christmas!" Ryan yelled back.

"Fucking loser," Justin said, and punched him in the arm. Then Ryan punched him back. Justin's muscles went from loose to tight in seconds, and it was then Ryan remembered Justin could hit you, but you could not hit him back.

"You're a fucking dead man," Stevie said.

Ryan took off running. Then they all did, racing around the church grounds like they had run around as boys. Ryan felt partly like Peter Pan and partly like Piggy from *Lord of the Flies*.

Carter and Justin were hard bodied, but their gym-built physiques slowed them down. Ryan was in the lead, Stevie a little behind him. Ryan had run the perimeter of the church grounds, he came around the corner and the light from the nativity drew him. He became convinced that this was like home in a game of tag. If he took shelter with the holy family, he himself would be safe. They would protect him, these enormous talismans.

Ryan stood beside Mary, catching his breath, and soon Stevie was beside him, looking down at Jesus and then Carter and Justin were beside them, catching their own breath. There was a moment of peace. Ryan was filled with a love of humankind. The festive spirit of good will towards all grew in him, until Justin reached into the manger and picked up Jesus. Justin laughed.

"What are we gonna do with you?" he asked the baby.

It was a step too far for Carter, he grabbed Jesus from Justin and tossed him to Stevie. Justin went for Carter, knocking over Joseph, who fell hard, and lay beside the wrestling men with his head at an odd angle. Carter escaped from Justin and ran out of the shelter; he grabbed the shepherd and stood behind him. When Justin lunged for him, Carter threw the shepherd down, the shepherd fell on his side. Carter darted between the wise men, toppling all three of them. Two fell face forward, the other flat on his back. Justin grabbed Carter and put him in a headlock. Stevie stood, still holding Jesus tentatively in front of him, hands under the tiny armpits, like he was a real baby someone had just passed to him to hold for a minute. Jesus's head was like an old-fashioned doll's, with hard wormlike curls of hair painted on. The siren went just twice, two audible exclamation marks, the loud bleep-bleep getting their attention.

"Stay where you are," a cop called out.

Carter and Justin came apart at the sound of the siren, and scurried like crabs out of the line of the light coming from the headlights of the police car, and then they ran. Ryan and Stevie looked like they were performing an abduction, the child's father, the shepherd, the wise men lay on the ground, the mother shocked and immobile staring at the empty crib, the baby was gripped in Stevie's hands.

"Fuck, Ryan, I'm on fucking probation," Stevie was crying. He looked at Ryan. Ryan looked at Jesus dangling from Stevie's outstretched hands. Ryan reached out and took the effigy from him and Stevie ran. Seconds later, the flashlight was in Ryan's eyes and the police found Ryan alone, cradling Jesus amongst the chaos.

FEATHERS

~

Joseph Finn has gone down to the funeral home to talk to the director, William Dooley, about his daughter. Victoria owes Joseph money. Usually, Joseph gets Kev to do this kind of work, but Joseph went to high school with William. Joseph used to sell William pot, and they had once skipped school and hot-boxed one of the hearses. The funeral for Joseph's mom had been at Dooley's Funeral Parlour.

William had been there. Even though he was still in high school, he was already part of the family business, used to wearing a black suit and opening doors to crying relatives. It was weird for Joseph to see him like that; at school he wore long shorts and a backwards baseball cap. But then

Joseph was wearing a suit that day too, and a tie that felt like it was choking him. William shook Joseph's hand, but unlike everyone else who had said a bland "I'm sorry for your loss," William leaned in close and whispered, "Fuck cancer. Fucking fuck cancer. I'm so sorry, man." It had been a relief to Joseph to hear someone echoing the anger he felt inside, instead of the bland acceptance. Even back then, when he was a teenager, he didn't believe his mom was in a better place.

William's daughter is in trouble. Joseph has seen it too many times: girls that one year are the most trusted of babysitters, who say their mom is their best friend, the next year they are rooting around in their grandmother's underwear drawer looking for jewelry they can sell, maxing out their parents' credit cards. You wouldn't trust them to cat sit, let alone look after a baby. They would forget where it was, or try and sell it on the dark web, or put it in the microwave. You hear about that bad shit happening. Joseph doesn't like seeing what happens to his customers, but if he doesn't supply them, someone else will.

Going to see William is a courtesy. Joseph suspects he has no idea how deeply lost his daughter is. She owes him $8,000. And, as Joseph finds himself saying to William, better she owes it to me than someone who will find other ways to make her pay. He's sure William doesn't want to think about that. Joseph knows he will think about it, and that William will pay up.

Joseph hasn't been to this building in a long time. The burgundy carpet and the dark wood of the entranceway smell of lemon Pledge. The office William has left Joseph waiting in has austere wooden panelling and a stained-glass window. The shafts of light hitting a corner of William's desk are coloured blue and green.

It hasn't changed much since his mom's funeral. The paint is fresh but the colours are the same. Joseph was sixteen when his mom died. He didn't cry during the funeral. He held his sister Carly's hand through the whole service, just like he had when they were little and his mom got him to hold Carly's hand when he walked her to school.

When Carly was six and he was eight, their mom woke them up on a cold night at the end of March and made them get out of bed. She tucked them up in the back of her car wrapped up in blankets. Joseph could tell his mom had been crying by the catch in her voice when she said his name. Carly was wearing a long blue cotton nightdress, like a long T-shirt. There was a silky strip of material around the neck and she rubbed it against her lips as they drove. Joseph thought they were going for good. Getting in the car and going on the run. He had heard his parents arguing earlier in the evening, raised voices and the sound of slamming kitchen cupboard doors had crept up the stairs and into Joseph's bedroom. Carly took his hand as soon as they got in the car and gripped it, her thumb worrying away at his, rubbing back and forth. Their mom didn't say anything, and her silence scared him. They didn't get on the highway but turned down the dirt road that headed to the lake. They went there in the summer sometimes, but in the winter the road was still thick with snow. Trees were crowded together on either side of the car; the only light came from a bright full moon.

Joseph was young, but still he heard bits on the news. Once when he was in the car with his father, he had half heard a story about a man driving his car off a bridge, with his two young children in the back seat. His father, noticing him listening, had switched the radio to a different station.

Joseph's mom drove them far down the road, away from the lights of houses and the sound of the occasional truck on the main road. She stopped and made Joseph and Carly get out of the back seat. Carly still gripped Joseph's hand. It was a windless night.

His mom put her finger to her lips to keep them quiet and then she released a long singing moan, an inhuman noise. It was full of beautiful sorrow. Joseph thought he was dreaming. He tried to wake himself up, but it didn't work. An owl, its large wings catching the moonlight, swooped down. It came so close they could feel the air it pushed down from its wings. It landed in a tree close to them and observed them. They could see its yellow eyes watching them. He didn't remember the drive home. When he woke up, he was tucked up in his bed, and Carly was snuggled up next to him.

"I can get you two thousand now, but the rest is going to take a while," William says.

"How long?" Joseph asks.

"I could give you a prepaid funeral."

This is desperate talk. Joseph has seen this before. "The thing is, my friend, for the moment, I am alive, you see, so a funeral does me no good. You owe me, and I owe people. And let me tell you, the people I owe, now they are not patient."

Joseph says this all reasonably. He discusses this business in a slow and easy style, similar to when he discusses waste-management contracts with town councillors and building contractors.

William makes an excuse about a delivery, to leave the room. Joseph knows there is no one waiting at the loading dock for William to sign for a shipment. William needs a minute to shit, or cry, or have a stiff drink to calm the panic he is now feeling. William deals with death every day, but even though he is used to seeing other people get smashed by tragedy, he wasn't expecting this. Joseph had told him he wanted to meet to talk about making some changes to the dumpster collection schedule. Finn's picks up the dumpsters behind the funeral home and replaces them three times a week with fresh ones. You can't have garbage stinking away behind a business such as William's. William was genuinely surprised when Joseph said, "Look, William, I'm here about your daughter." In some ways this is the best thing that could happen to Victoria, it gives her parents a chance to rescue her before she gets in any deeper. Joseph would want someone to tell him if his son was in trouble. Although, if anyone gave anything, even a joint, to his kid he would kill them.

There are school pictures on William's desk. William's kids, two boys and the daughter. Joseph's son plays hockey with the older son. The daughter is only fifteen. Too young. People like William, they think their kids won't get into the hard stuff. It does not matter what stats you throw in their faces; they think their children are too smart. But the drugs are everywhere. Go for a walk in the woods and you'll find an empty prescription bottle. Joseph has seen needles down by the beach. He's given his own son the riot act about never picking them up. He makes his garbage crews wear thick gloves.

You never really know what your children will get up to. Look at Joseph, he wanted to be a lawyer or a wrestler when he was a kid. For a little while, he wanted to be a radio host, like his dad. He even thought about becoming a cop. He came from a good family, that's what everyone said. His dad was small-town famous. Joseph's mom tempered his father's gambling habits, and things got fucked after she died.

Their dad was addicted to scratch tickets, all his savings gone, his fingernail always dirty with grey gunk. When Joseph found out (part of his dad's twelve steps was telling him and Carly) he had been disgusted. What a stupid addiction. There was nothing even cool about it, not like poker or heroin.

He had dipped into funds at work but they didn't fire him. He had a loyal following and the station didn't want the controversy. He claimed it was all a big misunderstanding, the grief had confused him. He remortgaged the house to pay back the money he owed and started going to Gamblers Anonymous.

The picture of William's daughter must be an old one. She looks to be about the same age Carly was when their mom got the cancer diagnosis. That winter, the trees in their garden were filled with evening grosbeaks, chickadees, goldfinches, juncos, sparrows, and redpolls. Sometimes the blue jays came and yelled at the smaller birds. Joseph loved the blue jays with their bright feathers and boldness, but their mom called them bullies and sent Carly out to chase them away. The squares of seed-studded suet attracted woodpeckers and flickers with their spotted yellow bodies. As a child Carly had called them polka-dot birds. The more colourful birds, with their flashes of red, blue and yellow, were the only colour outside that time of year. They were a relief from the glare of the white snow and the grey leafless trees. Joseph hung the feeders where his mom could see them. He filled them up every morning, early, before he went to school, and their mom would tell him and Carly about what she had seen when they got home. She had always loved birds. He could still identify them. Sometimes he would text Carly if he saw something good, a flock of cedar waxwings, a kingfisher on the electrical wires by the river, an osprey diving in the bay. She would text back a brief description of a recent sighting of her own, a pigeon on the sidewalk, or a cardinal in her neighbour's tree.

"I can write you a cheque for four now, but it's going to take a while to get the rest." William was shaking. Poor fuck, thought Joseph, but he knew better than to let his sympathy show.

"I'll tell you what. I'll come by with some invoices for some extra work I've done for you over the past month. You remember that work? And you can write me a cheque for that. And I'm sure by then you'll have found the rest of it. You need to talk to your wife. Get your kid in rehab. I'll come by Thursday, at three. Write that down now." He waits until William has written down the time and date. Not that he would forget, but Joseph wants to show William who is in control. That Joseph can make him do anything. He knows William will come up with the cash. Take out a loan if he needs to. Joseph feels for him, but what he said is true, he needs to pay the people he owes money to. And you don't get far in this business if you don't know how to collect debt. He is glad they can handle all this civilly. No need for baseball bats or emails suggesting they go on a hunting trip together.

Once, a hawk had killed a sparrow that was hanging out by his mom's bird feeders. She watched it happen. "You can't stop nature," Joseph remembered her saying. Carly cleaned up the kill site. She picked up the feathers that were left on the ground and kicked over the bloody snow, flipping over frozen hunks to hide the red stains. She kept the feathers in a jar. That night the three of them watched *The Birds* together. Carly pulling a blanket over her head at the scary parts and Joseph and his mom teasing her. Their dad wasn't home. Joseph could picture him parked in his car scratching away at ticket after ticket, feeling a rush when he won another one, the final crash when he was out of money, with no tickets left to scratch. Driving back to the office, telling himself no one would notice the money he borrowed from the safe. Telling himself he would pay it back.

Joseph is at his son's hockey game. William is there too. Joseph goes and stands beside him. Joseph sponsors a few teams. A Finn's Disposals banner hangs above the ice. William looks nervous, starts talking. "I was going to call you—"

Joseph stops him. "No business talk at the arena. That's my rule. It's good for all of us to take a break. We're here for the kids." He biffs William on the shoulder. Joseph's son looks up and waves at his dad in the bleachers.

The sky was like a blank bright screen on a television the winter Joseph's mom died. Either a monotone blue or a blinding white. During the day, it was like being in an interrogation room. The light leaking in the house was so bright it penetrated his mom's skin. The thinner she got, the more of her veins he could see. She started wearing sunglasses inside the house on all but the most overcast days.

The day before she went into hospital, the first robin of the year arrived. Joseph and Carly both sat on her bed and watched it with her.

Their mom's stay in hospital was brief, and everyone agreed this was a mercy.

When the weather really warmed up the spring that his mom died, his dad made Joseph take down all the feeders. He said they were attracting rats.

That summer Joseph started working for his uncle's company, Finn's Disposals. He got big, he towered over his dad and Carly. The physical work with his uncle and the weights he lifted in his uncle's garage changed him. He hung out with the men he worked with, guys in their twenties and thirties. He learned about garbage disposal from his uncle and about drug dealing from two of the men on the crew. When school started in September, he started dealing. It was fun money at first, but then it turned out he was good at it. He was the kind of guy people were happy to invite to parties: good looking, girls liked him. His size helped too, he looked intimidating, and it turned out, he was quite capable of inflicting violence.

Joseph moved out as soon as he was done high school. He bought a piece of land and started building his own house. He kept working for his uncle, and he kept up his other business too. Carly worked hard in high school, she closed herself up in her bedroom with her books. In the summer, she went birdwatching, getting up just before the sun and heading out early every morning. She found an eagle's nest and took pictures of it, lying down at a cliff's edge and pointing down with her camera. She told Joseph about it, and he told her he would come see it one day, but he never did. He had to get up early to drive the garbage truck and, on the weekends, he liked to sleep in.

Joseph shows up five minutes early for his meeting with William. There is a young guy working who ushers Joseph into the office and offers to make him a coffee. Joseph declines, he's pretty sure this is one of the embalmers fresh up from prepping some body when Joseph rang the doorbell on the funeral parlour's front door. Joseph picks up the picture of William's daughter, he's holding it when William comes in.

"How's she doing?" Joseph asks William.

William closes his eyes and shakes his head.

"She'll get through this. We'll get through it together." It sounds like someone, his wife maybe, has told him to tell people this. Joseph carefully puts the photo back in its place.

Joseph hands over a couple of invoices. Believable stuff. Who knew what kind of shit undertakers had to dispose of? No one was going to query a few high bills. Besides, he knew William used the same accountant as him. Keith

Cole appeared as straight as it gets, but he never asked questions about any of Joseph's receipts or less traditional investment habits. William's hands shake as he signs the cheques. He goes to the safe, Joseph politely averts his eyes as William works the combination lock. He listens to the clicks as William turns the dial.

The summer before Carly left for university, Peter Noseworthy died in a shed fire. Peter lived down the road from where Joseph was building his house. Every time Joseph got to work, Peter would come by and say, "You got a permit for that?"

Peter asked a lot of questions. "How'd a young guy like you make enough money to build your own house? You didn't get it from your dad, that much I know." Peter liked to gossip, he was a loudmouth. The kind of guy that thought he had something on everyone.

Peter kept gasoline in his shed, and he was a smoker. The volunteer fire department stopped the fire from spreading to his house, but it was too late for Peter.

When Joseph asked Carly to tell the police she was with him the night of the fire, she didn't hesitate. She never asked him where he had been.

Their dad couldn't help Carly out with university. He was deep in debt, and they both knew he was back at the gambling, believing in a win that never came. There had been some money that their mom had put aside for their education, but that had been scratched away too.

Carly paid her tuition in cash. Joseph gave her the wad of money. Ten thousand dollars in twenty-dollar bills, he told her to keep it in her mattress. She was finishing up her PhD the last year she accepted his money. Joseph visited her in Toronto. Carly showed him the underside of the futon she slept on. She had slit the futon along the seam and put the money inside, sewed it up so carefully no one would know it had ever been cut. They both got tattoos on that trip. Carly got a cedar waxwing on the inside of her wrist, and Joseph got an eagle on his bicep.

William hands Joseph a discreet envelope.

"There's a really good rehab place in New Brunswick. You should try and get her in there. Buddy of mine went, said it worked miracles," Joseph says to William. When he is leaving William's office the young guy from before is just coming up the stairs. "Good doing business with you, William," Joseph calls over his shoulder.

WE SMOKE OUR SMOKES

~

I start my day with nicotine. I love the feel of that first draw, the smoke going down my throat and giving me just the lightest head buzz. That first smoke baptizes my brain and clears out all the shit from yesterday.

I have another cigarette while I walk to work. We don't close for snowstorms, or hurricanes, or Christmas. People depend on us. When I get to the store, I unlock the door, count the float, and then I get on with it; I sell people what they need.

I got the local radio station on in the early morning. I know if the highway ramps are clear and if any roads are blocked with snow. I'll hear if the schools are closing.

If one of the cops or paramedics comes in after getting off their night shift, they tell me if there were any car accidents during the night, then I can let my customers know.

Most of my morning customers are polite. They're patient if I'm slow getting the cash up and running, or if I'm a few minutes late because I had to shovel my way out at home. We say good morning and talk about the weather in quiet voices. I've got a few I hate serving, mostly men, who hardly say a word to me and act like we don't see each other every day. Never a please or thank you. It doesn't matter that I know exactly who they are and I went to school with their mothers. They act like I'm a total stranger. I serve them in silence. They pay for their Canadian Classics, get in their trucks slamming their doors shut, and peel out of the parking lot lighting up at the same time.

The next little rush I get is kids coming for breakfast on their way to school: Jos Louis and a Pepsi, bag of chips and a chocolate milk. We have bananas and apples on the counter but they never take those. Around the same time, my drinkers arrive. We only sell beer and I can't sell any till eight-thirty. They wait around twitching until I can ring them through. A few of them get the shakes so bad they can't wait until they get home to have a drink. They down their first beer of the morning sitting in front of their steering wheel or half-hiding, leaning up against the back wall of the store out of view from the street. I pretend I haven't seen anything and pick up the bottles later.

Some will have been at it hard all night; won't stop until they pass out. When one of them doesn't show up for a few days we usually get a funeral notice to hang in the window.

I like it to be busy but not too busy. Not like the days when we get the delivery for beer and chips at the same time. The store's so small I have to stack the boxes in the aisle, and then I have to make sure no youngster (or middle-aged skeet) helps himself to a box of Doritos while I'm checking his nan's tickets. I don't get a real break, but I don't mind. I pop out now and then for a quick smoke. Mid-morning you only get a few customers. People run in for toilet paper, milk, a couple of break-opens and cigarettes. They like to gossip. "How's it going, Shannon?" they'll say, but they don't wait for a reply, just launch in about the weather and who's pregnant, or dead, or up to the hospital for chemo.

At noon, my cousin Brenda or one of the part-timers comes in. We get another run from the school at lunchtime; kids in for snacks and drinks. They all have a thing for jerky these days, and the weirder the flavour the more they seem to like it.

The afternoon is hard. It's when the boredom sets in. Brenda starts grating on my nerves. She talks too much about her daughter Evie and her plans for university. You'd think she was fucking Einstein the way Brenda goes on.

Me and Jerome don't have children. It just never happened. A couple of times my period was late and I had a little shimmer of excitement but then I started bleeding. We never talk about it. Brenda asked me once why we don't have kids. I told her to mind her own business then I went out for a smoke. We pretended like nothing had happened when I came back in.

I guess I must be infertile, I never went to the doctor to find out, all she ever wants to talk about is how come I haven't quit smoking yet. And it's not like we could afford any of those treatments. Brandy Dawe and her husband spent over twenty thousand on the mainland getting IVF. And now I'm in my forties. Old enough to be someone's nan and Jerome's stayed with me.

It's during the afternoon slump we get customers who hang around for too long. There are a few harmless old guys, they come in to buy milk or a newspaper they won't read. Mrs. Thorne comes in to buy food for the stray cats. It makes me sad how many people end up alone. I'll chat for a bit and then start moving stuff around when they need to go. They always get the message.

There's a few creepy ones who come sniffing around. The first few times old Tom Tobin came in he acted all innocent, but he was figuring out if I was alone. One day when Brenda was in the back, he hugged me. *He's just old and lonely*, I thought. But then a few days later, he hugged me again and this time his filthy fingers reached out and touched my bum and a little bit of my boob and I thought, *No, he can't be*. But he was.

When I complained to my boss, Gary, he said I was overreacting and it was all political correctness gone mad. "He just wants a little hug. He's never doing no harm," he said, like it was part of my job to get felt up by some old pervert every now and then. These days when I see old Tom coming, I get in behind the counter and pretend to be talking on the phone. Brenda crosses her arms over her chest when he shows up and grunts in response to any chit-chat.

At three, school's out: chocolate bars, chips, cans, jerky—the occasional smartass asking for cigarettes or trying to bring a case up to the counter.

Most evenings, I'm off at four. Every couple of weeks one of the part-timers calls in sick or quits. If it's me and Brenda working, she'll stay till close at 11 p.m. and I'll hang on until six so she gets her supper. If I'm working with one of the other girls, I always end up staying, even though I been in at work since 6 a.m. They always have some reason they can't stay: their mom needs her insulin shot, their husband's home from offshore, their back's hurting, they have to get their kids supper. I have reasons to go home too, but I stay. I guess I need this job more than them. I smoke a lot when I work nights. It helps calm my nerves.

I don't get put on night shifts regularly since I got held up. Gary's been pretty good about that. It doesn't happen very often here, everyone knows each other. In St. John's they get robbed all the time. Some hard case goes in with a knife, a syringe, a chainsaw, and wants the clerk to hand over money. Sometimes the cashier gets all foolish and refuses to hand anything over or they chase down the criminal after they've left. They think they're some kind of minimum-wage superhero. You see them on the news later, standing outside the store talking to reporters, acting all proud for wrestling down some alcoholic seventy-year-old who stole a pack of smokes and the butt end of a bologna.

After our store got hit, Brenda said she would have held on to the money. But she wasn't the one standing behind the counter looking at those crazy drugged-up eyes. That boy looked at me and I knew he would have used that box cutter to slit my throat if I didn't hand over everything in the till. Brenda would have ended up dead.

The police were good. Told me I done the right thing. Gary kept asking if I was sure I didn't recognize the perp. He used that word a lot that week like he thought he was on a detective show. "Shannon, you know everyone around here. Are you sure the perp didn't look familiar?"

I'm not foolish enough to make trouble over $275 and the beer the little fuck dropped. Stevie wasn't thinking straight when he grabbed those bottles. It's hard to make a fast getaway with a full case on your handlebars.

STEVIE DIES TWICE

~

Kev waits, drumming the steering wheel, while Carter does the pickup. Talk radio's on low, his nan's station. She gets mad if he ruins her perfect seat adjustment, or hip-hop music comes pouring out of the speakers and she has to search the airwaves to find VOCM after he borrows her car. He believes if he leaves everything just as his nan has, even if it means hugging the steering wheel as he drives, that the universe will protect him. Tinkering with the radio dial would be jinxing himself.

Nan's beige Corolla is the kind no one notices, even parked up behind the twenty-four-hour Sobeys in St. John's late on a Tuesday night. The kind of car some missus would drive to the store at one-thirty in the morning. Kev can picture this woman, an elderly insomniac, standing in her kitchen trying to pour milk into her tea and realizing the can is empty, or lying in the dark until the itch of her break-open addiction gets her up, and out of bed, believing the winning ticket is waiting under plexiglass at the seven-items-or-less checkout.

The radio plays "Onward Christian Soldiers." He and Carter, tonight they are soldiers, brothers in arms. Kev watches the Jeep. Everything seems okay. He'd made Carter take three deep breaths before going to meet the seller.

When he drives his own vehicle, a white Dodge Ram, Kev pumps out bass, making the tarmac beneath him vibrate, while he sits in parking lots waiting for Carter to come out of Subway, Tims, the liquor store. Once, Shane Tuck made the mistake of joking that Carter was like Kev's wife, but Kev wasn't having none of that. He broke Shane's nose, then Carter pushed Shane down and kicked him until he mewled and spat blood. Kev pulled Carter away when he saw two teeth on the ground. People had to learn respect, but Carter could overdo it.

Kev watches Carter get out of the Jeep, slow and steady. He keeps his limbs loose, like Kev taught him. Kev wishes Carter had backed away from the Jeep, not turned his back on it so soon. Kev feels an empathetic tightening of his own back muscles. Reaching his hand over, he rests it on the latch of the glove compartment. Slowly. He doesn't want to unnerve the other dealer. Nothing happens. Carter walks across the lot. The Jeep is only twelve spaces away, but it is like time slows down for the journey. Carter gets in the passenger seat beside Kev and exhales.

The Jeep is too showy for Kev's liking. Black with Quebec plates. It looks like a drug-dealer's car, and that's fine for driving around when you aren't carrying product or protection, but not okay when you're actually working. The Jeep revs up its engine, and instead of pulling out of the lot quietly, it peels out of its spot and comes right past the Corolla. The passenger peers in at Kev with a shit-eating grin. Kev can't make out much of his face, just the gold tooth glinting. The guy has a baseball cap pulled low over his eyes.

"Fucking Frenchy faggots. What they think this is? Fucking amateur hour?" Kev says.

"Y'wants me to buy something?" Carter asks.

Kev usually sends Carter into the store to buy something after they get their product—diapers, or kid's Aspirin. The kind of stuff a guy's baby momma would send him to pick up, late on a Tuesday in September.

"Maxi-pads. And get me a cold plate too. Make sure it's got the beet salad."

"You serious, Cocky? You expect me to buy that bitch stuff like I'm on the rag?"

"Get those and some chocolate and it will look like wifey sent you."

"Look like I'm whipped."

"Just do it," Kev says quietly, and Carter gets out of the car.

Kev doesn't know why, but he has a feeling about that shit-eating grin. He'd convinced Joseph this was a good connection, and if there is trouble, well, Joseph doesn't like trouble.

"Coke," Joseph told him when he was learning, "is easy money. Dangerous to get in, but man, it's a seller's market. Everyone loves coke. The lawyers love it, the artists like it, the guys from the oil fields. No class to coke, it isn't a skeet drug, or a hipster drug, or a businessman's drug. All the world loves coke."

And that was the deal Kev had set up. A guy Carter met inside. It was his brother from Montreal they were buying from; a new contact and one he hopes is going to impress the shit out of Joseph. Joseph is looking more and more legit, using guys Kev doesn't know. Guys who blend in wherever they are, and look like they work for Newfoundland Power or Canada Post, and some of them do. But Kev knows Joseph needs him and his public face. Kev is like Joseph's mascot, the one that people have bad dreams about when they owe Joseph money and imagine creeping in through their windows when they think about calling the cops to report suspicious activity happening in Joseph's shed or down at the dock.

Carter doesn't like needles, doesn't have any ink, and that is part of why Kev sends him into stores and across parking lots. He is less memorable. Carter had been on the news when he was up on assault charges, a picture of him in the dock made the paper, but no one ever recognized him. Carter was clean shaven and kept his hair short; his neck showed his workouts. He usually wore a thick gold chain but his lawyer made him take it off in court. Carter looked like any guy who'd grown up in the bay, or the Pearl, and made money and muscle out in Alberta. A hard ticket, but not necessarily criminal.

Kev knew his ink scared the shit out of people. Just a look at his face was enough to get what he wanted. He had tats over his shoulders and upper arms, right up under his chin. Above his left eye, the word *Purity*. His nan called him Jam Jam when he was a kid after his favourite Purity brand cookies. It's a nod to her, and the result of a brief flirtation with some white supremacists he met his first time inside. But the drug trade is multicultural, and he's now quick to explain the sentimental reason for the word. The other tattoos on his face are a heart and a bone coming down like tears from his right eye. The heart is for his sister, Annabelle, who died of a heart condition when she was three. The bone is for his dead dog, an Irish setter named Whiskey.

Driving home from St. John's after the pickup, Kev is still listening to his nan's station. Carter is amped. His leg jiggles, he keeps turning around in his seat and checking the rear window, but it's two in the morning and the highway is empty. The cops out here go home at midnight, only get called out if there's trouble.

"Can we change the station, Cocky? I need something with a beat."

"Don't you got your phone?"

Carter shrugs, pulls a pair of earbuds out of his hoodie. He looks down at his phone, and starts texting. Kev can hear the music leaking from Carter's ears.

"You'll go deaf, my son." But Carter doesn't hear him.

The radio station Kev has on is replaying highlighted interviews from the day before. Kev finds himself listening to a conversation about Use Safe, US, a drug-safety organization in St. John's. US is complaining that the government won't bring in fentanyl testing strips to Newfoundland and Labrador. The strips allow users to test their drugs before they use. You can order them online, but US can't hand them out. They are handing out naloxone kits, which can reverse an overdose if administered correctly.

"But don't you feel this is just contributing to the problem?" the interviewer asks. "Condoning drug use. Wouldn't the government be better off going after the dealers?"

The idea comes to him as he rotates his middle finger upwards, this is one of those fortuitous moments, one of those fateful coincidences that remind Kev he is special. He hasn't fucked with his nan's car, and the universe has rewarded him. He doesn't have enough time to order any strips, but he can get one of those naloxone kits for free. All he needs is a guinea pig, a fucking canary in the coal mine. He glances over at Carter, but no, he can't do that. Kev loves his boys.

Joseph will kill him if he brings a bad batch into the region. It's a small town, a small province, and Joe doesn't like too much attention brought to the business. If a customer overdoses, that means attention.

Joseph's other soldiers, the ones that are hiding in plain sight, some of them are the kind of men who can make you disappear. Last year, the town's bylaw officer became way too interested in the trailers parked up at the back of Joseph's property. Demanded permits. Wanted to see inside. A few days later, he died when his truck went off the side of the highway. His power steering failed. And Peter Noseworthy, rumour had it, he was cracking jokes at the Legion: "Joseph Finn's the richest garbageman I ever seen." Days later Peter's shed burned with him inside it.

Carter had been texting for most of the ride home. "Better not be our business you're talking 'bout," Kev says loud enough for Carter to hear. Carter turns his screen towards Kev, and when Kev glances over, he sees the exchange is between Carter and his kid sister. Making plans for her birthday party. Carter stops texting and puts the phone down. "Mom just caught Evie still awake, and on her phone, and took it off her. But she got Evie to text me first to tell you to drive safe."

They get off the highway and roll down the main street into Bay Mal Verde. The lights are out in most of the houses, just the occasional glow of blue screen where someone either couldn't sleep, or has fallen asleep in the living room, not wanting to join whoever they share a bed with. Barrelling down the other side of the street towards them, the engine growling wildly, the driver helmetless, comes a three-wheeler.

"Stevie Loder," Kev says out loud when the ATV passes them. Kev feels like the universe is rewarding him again.

"Fucking faggot," Carter says, turning his head to see Stevie turning onto the highway on his ancient machine. The ATV backfires and both Carter and Kev laugh.

"Fucking Stevie, where'd he get that piece of shit from?" Kev asks.

"His nan's fucking panty drawer, most likely."

Kev laughs too much at Carter's reply. It wasn't that funny. Carter isn't good at funny.

"Carter, my son. Carter, I got an idea. Tomorrow afternoon you and me are heading back to town. Bring your sister. I'll buy her lunch at the mall."

"Cocky, I don't want Evie getting mixed up in nothing. She's only fifteen."

"Nothing illegal. I swear. I just needs her to do me a little favour."

"Cocky, I don't know. If Mom..."

"Fuck. Just trust me, man. Nothing's gonna happen to your little sister. We'll take her for lunch at the mall. I'll buy her a present after. One of them crystal bracelets, or them charms, from the place by the food court. I know what girls like. I just need one small favour."

"If you get Evie in trouble, I'll kill ya." Carter's voice hardens up, like it does just before he loses control and starts pounding someone.

"I know, man. It's all good. I know she's just a kid. Nothing bad's going to happen."

~

Kev insists Evie sits up front and Carter sits in the back. The drive takes just over an hour. Evie doesn't say much, just glances at Kev when she thinks he doesn't notice. He tells her stories, the kind of stories girls like, about going fishing with his pop when he was a kid. She looks scared shitless when they pull up outside the place in St. John's. The Use Safe office is inside a shelter for homeless youth, and despite the sunflowers painted on the outside, it is rough and institutional. Kev gives Evie a little pat on the knee before she gets out of the car. Nothing overt, just enough to make her feel special.

Three teenage skeets are standing around outside of the shelter. They start looking Evie up and down as soon as she gets out of the vehicle. Kev opens the door of his truck. He leans his head and shoulders out and stares at the teenagers. One glance at his face and they avert their eyes real fast. Two of them quickly stub out cigarettes. The other pockets his vape.

Evie is wearing one of those pink fluffy sweatshirts and yoga pants. Kev lets his eyes linger where the young skeets' had. Her pants keep slipping over her hips revealing white smooth skin that Kev wants to stroke and cover up at the same time.

"Still legend," Carter says from the back seat of the car. He is watching the kids take off, not Kev's lingering gaze.

Half an hour later, Evie is back in the truck with a zip-up pouch containing a naloxone kit, a plastic bag full of pamphlets on safe drug use and addiction services, and, Kev notices, although he doesn't mention this in front of Carter, a bunch of condoms and little packages of lube. They are just like the packets you get ketchup in.

~

They are sitting at a table in the food court at the mall. Evie has a smoothie with goji berries and soy milk. Carter takes a sip and makes gagging noises. He goes to get some fries. Kev's phone vibrates. He looks at the number then answers his phone. "Yep, buddy," he says every thirty seconds, but mostly he listens and watches Evie.

"Evie, y'done real good," he says as he gets off the phone.

"Thanks, Kev." She looks him in the eye for the first time. He reaches out from where he's sitting across from her, and pushes the hair that falls over her face behind her ear. Then Kev notices Carter, a few feet from the table, holding a tray, staring at them. Carter's lip twerks up. Kev has seen that twist in Carter's mouth before when he put his fist through Jenny's window, and when he broke the end off a beer bottle and held it up to Craig Learner's throat.

"I got to make some calls." Kev gets up and slopes out towards the main doors of the mall. He lights up a smoke outside, and takes out his other phone, and texts his mom.

– *Needs anything from town?*

– *Im good bless u for asking* <3

He texts his mom a picture of a puppy holding a heart between its paws. When he goes back inside, Evie and Carter aren't talking. Evie is concentrating on sucking up her smoothie. Carter is turned away from Evie. He is slowly eating his fries, one at a time.

"Come on, Evie, let me buy you a little present for helping out," Kev says.

"She don't need one," Carter says and Evie, embarrassed, says, "No need, b'y," so Kev leaves it.

~

A couple of days later, Kev is parked on the road in front of the high school waiting for Carter to text him that he's found Stevie. He sees Evie, with some guy, walking on the other side of the street. The guy is skinny, wearing a black puffer jacket, undone, practically slipping off his shoulders, and white running shoes. Kev doesn't know him. His cheeks have red blotches, like he is a little kid, and Kev can't tell if this is from emotion or the cold. Something about those red blotches gets on Kev's nerves. Kev has the urge to get out there and hit the kid, harden him up a little. By the time Kev was that age, he was already doing time in Whitbourne. They stop and Evie turns to face Apple Cheeks. Fast words are forming on his lips, and then Apple Cheeks gestures in frustration. Evie turns on her heel and walks away fast. She is heading closer to Kev's truck.

Kev starts up his engine, rolls down his window and calls out, "You okay, girl? Wants a ride?" Evie sees him across the street. She is dewy eyed, but without her face all contorted, and Kev likes this about her. He hates when women get ugly when they weep, but Evie is pretty in her sadness. Kev doesn't wait for her to answer. He pulls his truck around in a fast U-turn and rolls up beside her. Evie pulls open the passenger door. As she closes it, Apple Cheeks calls out her name, "Evie," an adolescent crack in his voice. Evie turns towards her window, but Kev pulls out and doesn't give her a chance to change her mind. In his rear-view mirror, Kev sees the stupid kid crying, wiping snot from his nose with the back of his hand.

"Boyfriend?" Kev asks her and Evie shrugs.

"Wants to be," she replies, trying to sound hard.

Kev's phone buzzes and he glances down at an incoming text. "I just got to pop into my mom's and drop off her groceries, then I'm meeting Carter and a few of the b'ys at my place. I can take you straight home after Mom's."

Evie sighs. "I wish Carter was at home, then Mom could get on his case instead of mine."

"Mudder on the rag?"

Evie laughs. "Something like that."

"Come over and hang with the b'ys for a bit."

Evie nods.

Kev tries to remember what birthday Evie has coming up, sixteen or seventeen. He could ask Carter, but he doesn't want no hassle. He likes this girl, so much less work than friggin' Karen and Marina, both of them always with a smoke hanging out their mouths, always reeking of perfume and with pussies so bald they remind him of plucked chickens. Evie smells clean, he bets she wears cotton underwear, he bets she is still natural down there, maybe just a home-done landing strip.

Kev pulls into his mom's driveway. He gets out of the truck and grabs a plastic Dominion bag and a bucket of salt beef from the back seat. Evie is still seated in the truck, but Kev taps on the window.

"Come on in. Mudder'll want to see you. She loves Carter."

The front door isn't locked and when they go through two small dogs come rushing out. One, a Shih Tzu with a pink bow in her hair, bares her teeth at Evie. The other dog is a tiny black poodle. It gets so excited when Evie walks in, it pees all over the floor. Shirley Babcock comes out to greet her son. She drops an old towel on the floor and pushes it around to sop up the urine. The foot she uses to do this is clad in a fluffy slipper made to look like a pink flamingo, a protruding, and slightly floppy, head grows from its toes.

"Don't mind Panda and Teddy, they won't hurt you. Who's this then?" The question is slightly accusatory.

"This is Evie, Mom, Carter's sister."

"Evie, my God, girl, I've not seen you since you was a toddler. I see your mom all the time up to the Ultramar. Kevin, put my groceries in the kitchen. God loves ya. You need a shower. And change that shirt. You been wearing that since Sunday. I done your laundry and put it in your old room. Come with me now, girl, I'll make us a cup of tea."

Evie looks around at Kev, but he just shrugs. "You go on, Evie, while I freshen up."

"Thanks, Mrs. Babcock," she says taking the mug of tea.

"So nice to have some female company for a change. Well, Panda's a bitch, but that hardly counts. Ha, I'm friggin' shocking. Don't mind me, girl."

The litany of questions comes, but Evie is used to this. Mrs. Babcock needs to find out where Evie fits into the jigsaw of local genealogy and politics. She wants to know who Evie's friends are, and then tries to work out in what way she, Shirley Babcock, knows or is related to them, and then once she's made these inquiries, she pronounces, "You're a good girl."

Kev comes into the kitchen. Dressed and rubbing a towel over damp hair. He drapes his arms around his mom's shoulders, and she reaches round and kisses him on the cheek.

Carter and Stevie are already at Kev's place when he and Evie show up. They are standing on the porch. Stevie smoking, and Carter doing standing push-ups against the porch's rail.

"What the fuck, Cocky?" Carter says as he sees Evie heading towards him.

"That's no way to speak to your sister, b'y."

"Kev picked me up. I had a fight with Riley."

"Course you did. What you do, steal his My Little Pony?" Carter says to her.

Kev hugs Carter, banging Carter's shoulders with his fists. "Just coming to the rescue of a damsel in distress. Knew you'd want me to protect your kid sis, bro."

Stevie says nothing, just tilts his chin up at Evie, practically flicking off the Chicago Bulls hat he has perched on his head.

There are three locks on Kev's door. The others wait while he punches the code into his security system.

The place is clean, spotless even, and this surprises Evie. There is a brown sectional couch, a huge flat-screen TV mounted on the main wall, and an array of video games arranged on a bookshelf. There is another screen, the size of a small TV, on the other wall. It is one of those digital picture frames; Evie's eye catches a picture of Carter and Kev when they were kids, in baseball uniforms, and an older picture, that Kev must have scanned in, of a little girl with blond hair sitting on what must be, Evie realizes, Mrs. Babcock's knee.

"Have a seat, Evie. Me and the b'ys got a bit of business to do." Kev goes to the kitchen and comes out with a can of Pepsi, and a glass full of ice, and puts them next to Evie. He didn't ask her if she wanted it. "B'ys." He ushers Stevie, who has seated himself on the opposite side of the couch from Evie, up and away towards a door that Evie presumes is a bedroom.

"You okay out here?" Carter asks.

"Best kind," she says, imitating their mother's voice. Carter rumples her hair.

The curtains are drawn in the bedroom, but the bed is made. It takes up most of the room. It is king sized with a dark wood headboard, made up with red satin pillows and comforter. At the foot is a pastel quilt that Kev's nan made as a coming-home present, after he'd been sent to New Brunswick for two years of federal time. Kev gestures for Stevie to sit on the bed and he does. Stevie is looking around, looking scared. Hasn't been in Kev's bedroom since they were eight and Kev tied him up and shaved off his eyebrows. Well, he only got one done before Shirley Babcock caught Kev at it. She had tore a strip off Kev first, threatened to shave off his eyebrows, before she untied Stevie.

Carter stands by the door. He has his car keys in his hands and keeps twirling them around on his finger.

"Am I in trouble, Cocky? I not been skimming. I swear," Stevie says.

"I know you been skimming, but I don't care about that, long as I gets what you owe me. This is something different I wants to ask you about. Now, you don't have to do this, b'y, I wants you to understand, but I need a favour."

Stevie looks at Carter standing guard at the door, he feels the silk of the comforter with his fingers. Cocky said he didn't have to, but he sure feels like he has to do whatever it is he is asking. He hopes Cocky doesn't want him to kill any animals. Stevie likes animals.

"You don't want me to kill no dogs!" Stevie blurts it out, can't help himself.

"For fuck's sake, Stevie, why'd'ya think that? I loves dogs, b'y. Remember Whiskey? Remember how I used to let him ride round in the front of the truck and make Cindy sit in the back?"

"I remember that," Stevie says.

"Okay now, Stevie, I got some new product in, and I need to do a little quality control test. I know you likes to sample your own wares, and I need an expert. But I don't know a lot about this stuff, so if you're willing to try it, I'll get my boy Carter here to sit with you. Babysit you for a bit when you have a little free trial. But only if you wants to. I can't say for sure what kinda ride this stuff will give you, b'y."

Kev gets out the clear plastic bag, and as soon as he sees the white powder, Stevie starts licking his lips. "I'll check it out for you. I can tell you if it's the good stuff."

Kev hands Stevie a flat book, *The Children's Illustrated Bible*. His father's mother gave it to him when he was born. He takes out his wallet and almost hands Stevie a five and then decides that looks cheap, so he hands him a twenty instead. "You can keep that too. I don't want it after it's been covered in your snot."

"Thanks, Cocky," says Stevie, but his eyes are all for that white pouch of powder. Kev walks towards the door. He puts his hand on Carter's shoulder and pulls the naloxone kit out of his pocket. Carter nods at him. Kev goes out into the living room where he finds Evie, staring at the electronic picture frame, watching pictures of his life, bored.

"Sorry we was so long. Figured you'd be on your phone making up with your little boyfriend."

"Mom took my phone for the week since she caught me texting Carter after midnight. And he's not my boyfriend."

Kev turns on the TV, starts flipping through the channels, he stops on HGTV. *Bahamas Life* is on.

"I loves this show. One day I'm gonna live in one of those places, stay here for the summer, but come the fall I'll be by the beach down south, drinking out of a coconut," Kev says.

"You'll never. Wouldn't you get homesick? All the way out there with none of your people around."

"I'd bring 'em with me, girl. Can't you see my mom out on the beach in a string bikini?" Carter busts out of Kev's bedroom.

"Fuck! Fuck! Fuck! He's fucking dying in there, Kev."

"Use the stuff."

"I'm trying, I'm trying, man," Carter's hands are shaking too hard, and the kit in his hand jumps around his body. He hates needles.

Evie gets up and grabs it from him. "Give it to me," she says, and she is through the bedroom door before either of them can stop her. By the time Kev pushes past Carter's frozen form, Evie has the syringe prepped and jabs the thing right through Stevie's jeans, and into his thigh, then depresses the plunger. Doesn't even flinch as she drives the needle into his flesh. Evie turns Stevie into the recovery position all calm. Carter is crying in the doorway now, and Kev is pacing back and forth in the room. "Fuck, fuck."

"How come he's not coming around?" Kev asks her.

Evie gives instructions. "Just wait, it can take a few minutes. You need to call 911. This might not work and he needs an ambulance." She turns back to Stevie, but neither Kev nor Carter pull out their phones. She eyes them again after a minute, but before she can speak Carter does: "Hang on, he's coming round."

Stevie is pale and dazed but his eyes are moving around, and he is trying to sit up.

"Just take it easy now," Evie says and puts her arm around Stevie's shoulders trying to calm him as he jerks wildly.

"Fuck man, Stevie! You gave us some scare," Kev says. Carter has his back turned to the rest of them. He is facing the wall, wiping his eyes.

"Can I try that stuff now?" Stevie says, his gaze falling across the half-filled packet abandoned on the bed.

"One of you needs to call 911," Evie says.

"Fuck no, man, don't be calling the cops. I don't want any cops." Stevie is shaking his head.

"We need to call an ambulance to make sure you're alright, that's all," Evie tells him.

"You stupid, girl? You calls 911, the cops come whether you want them or not." Stevie is shaking Evie's arms off him. "Why you calling the fucking pigs, you fucking crazy?"

"You watch your manners, Stevie. That girl just saved your life," Kev says.

"You need to call an ambulance," Evie says again.

"We will Evie, God's honest truth, but first we needs to get you outta here. Can you walk home? Once you're gone, Carter and me will call an ambulance for Stevie, and keep you outta this shit." Kev is thinking things out as he is talking.

"Mom will fucking kill me if she knows you was here," Carter adds.

"You'll call once I'm gone."

"I swear," says Kev.

She hesitates at the door of Kev's house, even looks around for a land line, but of course there isn't one.

"Don't forget to phone!" she yells before she steps outside.

"Get going, Evie!" Kev shouts. He's never used this voice on her before. It isn't a voice you disobey.

Carter and Kev are in the living room taking counsel, pictures of beaches, palm trees and massive houses play on the screen behind them. Kev has muted the sound.

"We could drop him off at the hospital," Carter whispers.

"He seems fine," Kev says. "We can just keep him here for a couple of hours, keep an eye on him."

Stevie comes stumbling out of the bedroom, pulling on his ripped St. John's IceCaps jacket.

"Stevie, whadda y'at, b'y? You just got back from the dead. Why don't you sit for a while, take a load off?" Kev says.

"Whadda y'mean, back from the dead?"

"You was practically dead and then you came back, like Jesus!"

"I never. I don't remember none of that."

"You didn't see the light then? Or them flames? Well, that's a good sign." Kev laughs. It is forced laughter.

Stevie starts heading towards the door, but Carter gets in his way. He stands tall and solid directly in front of Stevie. Stevie flinches back from Carter. "Get outta my way! Cocky, tell him to move."

"You sure you feel alright, Stevie?" Kev asks him.

"Best kind."

Kev stares at Stevie. Then looks up at the TV screen and watches blue sky, sun, and sand for a full minute.

"Let him go," Kev says. He doesn't look at Stevie again. Carter moves out of Stevie's way.

~

The three-wheeler bucks as Stevie goes up the trail that leads from the back of Kev's place up into the woods. He is trying to wrap his head around what has happened. He'd OD'd, he'd died, and somehow that girl had brought him back to life. He doesn't remember none of it. He is heading to the clearing where he likes to go and think.

Stevie bumps along the trail. His ears go fuzzy after he rides because the engine on his machine is so loud, but he likes the jerk of it, the way it tosses him around like a ride at the fair, not like those new ATVs where you can hardly feel the ground under you. Stevie feels the roots and ruts he drives over.

People have partied up at the clearing for years. It is on top of the ridge that runs around the harbour. If you drew a straight line up from the old Catholic basilica, you'd end up here, in this space in the middle of the woods, where the rock is too close to the surface, so no trees grow. The clearing is surrounded by thick forest on all sides, and away from houses and prying eyes. Thousands of pieces of broken glass litter the ground, and underneath grow red partridgeberry. There is a ring of chairs made from the old seats of cars around a firepit. One of the car seats is burnt out and is just a blackened metal skeleton. Someone has recently set off fireworks, and the multicoloured remains of these lie scattered amongst the usual beer caps and shotgun shells. You can make out the word *Kaboom!* on one of them still. There is a huge boulder, the top of which is often covered with shot-up beer bottles, but Stevie knows when you stand on top of it, you can see right out into the Atlantic.

Stevie pulls up in the clearing, and gets off his three-wheeler. He takes a breath of the clean, cold air. He can smell the peat he's churned up on the trail, the smell of rot on fallen leaves and the burning smell of oil from his machine. The sun catches the broken bits of glass and the ground glitters green, amber and white. Stevie is back from the dead, he throws his arms up, the enormity of what has just happened to him filling him up.

"I'm like fucking Jesus!" he yells into the open space, and then the fentanyl hits him a second time.

MAN TIME

~

Ray didn't pick Kev up in one of his regular rides, a beat-up black Mustang, or the old truck he didn't have insured but used on the back roads. He arrived in a borrowed grey minivan. He was wearing black jeans and his workboots. He hadn't shaved for a couple of days.

"Car's in the shop," he said when Shirley asked.

"Whose van is it?" Shirley probed, but Ray shrugged her off.

"Just a guy I know. Stop being so nosey. Where's your kid at?"

Shirley narrowed her eyes a moment at her brother. Before Kev left, she pulled him in for a hug and looked at Ray over his shoulder. "Take care of him," she said to Ray.

"Jesus, Shirley. We're going to St. John's not to Afghanistan."

"Jesus, Mom," Kev echoed. Shirley did not smile.

They drove out of Bay Mal Verde and towards St. John's. Kev contemplated what snacks he might order at the movie theatre. Ray was the kind of uncle who would one day order you only a small pop, but the next time might get you candy, popcorn, a drink and upsize it all. Kev was hoping that Ray was in an upsize kind of mood. Ray was blasting Eminem as he drove, he knew all the words and tapped the steering wheel. When they got to town, he turned off the CD. They drove past the mall and onto one of the residential streets around it.

"What movie we gonna see?" Kev asked. Even as he hoped, Kev felt the disappointment coming. The reality of popcorn turning into an unfulfilled desire. He imagined the smell of butter, the salt and grease on his fingers, the hard burnt kernels at the bottom of the tub.

"Kev, my son. I got a surprise for you," Ray said.

The house was a bungalow, neat and well kept, but with no frills. All the houses on the street were the same. Flat lawns, the snow recently melted and revealing yellow grass. Beige or grey vinyl siding. This one had a front window divided into diamonds with white lines. There was a Christmas wreath on the door, all its once-green foliage now dead. Ray pulled a black beanie onto his head and dragged a clipboard out of the back seat.

"I'm gonna go up to the front door, pretend I'm delivering something. But first you are going to break in there and let me in."

Ray pointed out the window he wanted Kev to crawl through. A basement window at the side of the house, a half one.

"The guy that lives here is outta town. No need to worry about him."

Kev looked at his uncle, then he looked at the house. It was dusky out now. The light fading, it was quiet on the street. Seagulls were pecking at a split garbage bag a few houses down. It must have been out there all day and no one had cleaned it up yet.

"I ain't no thief," Kev said.

"Huh?" Ray shook his head at Kev. "We're not stealing. I'm just taking what I'm owed." Ray gestured towards an empty-looking hockey bag in the back seat.

"Take that with you. If anyone stops you, say you're looking for your friend that lives around here. Make up a name. Is this Johnny's house? Say that. There's a box cutter in there, you can use it to cut the screen."

Kev didn't need it. The screen was already detached in one corner, like a cat had been scratching it, and he just ripped the rest of the screen out. The inside window was unlocked like Ray said it would be. He shoved the hockey bag through first, then Kev sat with his feet dangling into the basement, lay back, and wormed the rest of his body in. He knocked something down with his feet and froze half in half out, listening, expecting someone to grab him by the ankle, but nothing happened. He felt vulnerable, his head and shoulders out in the open and his legs dangling into the unknown. He panicked and started squirming in fast, the back of his hand caught on a sharp edge of the aluminum screen. It stung and he could tell it was going to bleed. He kept going and then he was mostly in, his hands gripping the window frame and his legs hanging down. He let go and launched himself in. He landed on his feet and ran quick as he could up the stairs, down the hallway, and unlatched the deadbolt on the front door.

"Took your time," Ray said as he stepped inside holding the clipboard in one hand and glancing quick behind him. In the front hall was a low table with two porcelain figurines on it, a ballerina and a woman holding a flowery umbrella. Kev's mom would have loved them. There was a glass candy dish full of hard candies. Ray swept this all to the floor, laughing as they fell. The head of the ballerina broke off and rolled past Kev. He thought he saw her eyes blink at him. Ray walked downstairs and straight to a gun cabinet Kev hadn't had time to notice. Ray took out a drill from his bag and started drilling at the lock, the basement filled with a hot-metal smell. The drill whined and Ray swore at the cabinet calling it a bitch, a cunt, and a motherfucker. Kev's eyes adjusted to the dark and he saw what he had knocked over, one of those white Christmas reindeer made up out of twigs. It lay on its side like it was dead.

Kev licked blood off the back of his hand where it had formed into jammy beads. There was a plaque on the wall that said *World's Greatest Grandfather* and another that said *Man Cave*. There was also a Budweiser poster with a bunch of women in bikinis washing a car. Ray caught him staring at it. "I got some better pictures than that for you, son. When we get back to my place, I'll show you some real nice magazines."

There were three rifles in the cabinet and a hunting knife. Ray tossed them in the big hockey bag. They shoved the bag out the window Kev had come in from, then Ray gave Kev a leg up and told him to wait and count to three hundred then to come find Ray.

"Slowly like. One thousand, two thousand, three thousand... like that. Then come meet me around the corner."

Kev lay on the ground feeling cold and shivery. He heard Ray shut the front door, a subdued thud. He imagined he was a soldier lying in the trenches. He forgot to count. He heard a dog bark next door and then he took off looking for Ray. The hockey bag banged against his leg and he felt the sore ache of a bruise forming. The van was just around the corner, where Ray said it would be. Ray stayed in the driver's seat and Kev struggled opening up the sticky door and lifting the bag in.

When Kev finally got the bag in, Ray pulled out and pretended he was driving off. He stopped a few seconds later. Kev raced forward, and Ray pulled forward again. A car came down the street towards them and Ray kept the van still as Kev got in the front seat. "Your face!" Ray kept saying and chuckling. Then he offered Kev one of the hard candies he had knocked to the floor. It was red and cracked into pieces beneath its cellophane wrapper. It had sharp edges.

On the way home they passed a cop car on the highway. Ray laughed and turned up his music.

When they got to Ray's house, his Mustang was in his drive. Ray sent Kev in with the hockey bag. He told Kev he had to return the van.

"Put the bag under my bed. Do not open it. If anyone knocks on the door ignore it. Nobody is home. Got it? You did good today, kid."

As soon as he heard Ray pull out of the driveway, Kev opened the bag and took out one of the guns. He pointed it at the ceiling, at the TV, and at it his own reflection in the big gold-framed mirror Ray's ex-girlfriend had hung on one wall of the living room. There was a crack running across the glass in the top corner. When Ray got back, Kev was on the couch watching TV. The guns were tucked in under Ray's bed.

Kev spent time with Ray about once a month. "Your uncle called," his mom would say. "Man Time on Saturday."

Sometimes they would go see a movie, or Ray would rent one. He liked action movies starring men with machine guns. Other times they would head out for a drive. That's what Ray used to say. "Let's go for a drive, my son."

Occasionally, Ray had a plan, a specific house. "Buddy owes me." Often, they would just tour around different towns looking for opportunities.

"If people don't care about their stuff, they don't deserve it. The same is true for women. If Buddy isn't looking after his woman properly, you know what I mean by looking after? Course you do. He doesn't deserve her. She's fair game."

It was amazing what people kept in unlocked sheds. Once, Kev was wheeling a snow blower, brand new, out of a shed when a station wagon pulled up in the drive. Kev hid behind the shed; he could see Ray parked across the street. A whole family got out of the car, a man, a woman, two kids. They were close enough Kev could hear them talking, the guy was saying, "I wish you wouldn't tell your mom so much stuff. I don't even know if I'll get an interview for that job and she was asking me about it." They didn't notice their snow blower sitting in the middle of their green lawn at 9 p.m., where it had no business being.

Kev waited until the family was inside then he wheeled that snow blower right over the lawn and out of the yard to Ray. Kev imagined the family taking off their boots, the mom yelling at the kids to hang their jackets up and, all the while, Kev was taking away their snow blower like he owned it. He wanted to go back for a chainsaw he had seen, but Ray flicked his ear. "Don't get too fucking cocky, kid, that's how you get caught."

Ray started taking pills for his back. The pills made his eyes glossy. Money went missing from Kev's nan's purse. The silver spoons she got given at her wedding and her dead husband's watch disappeared. One night, Kev's mom wouldn't let Ray in their house and he stood at the outside, crying and then yelling. He banged on the door with his fists. Kev heard him call out, "Kev, my little man, let your uncle in, little buddy."

Shirley hammered back on the inside of the door with her own fists. "Get out of here now, Ray, or I'll call the cops. You knows I will if I have to."

None of them saw Ray for a few months, then he turned up for Sunday dinner and Kev's nan set a place for him, and said nothing. After dinner, Ray said, "Man Time!" and ushered Kev towards his truck. Kev's mom and nan exchanged glances, but they didn't stop Kev from going with Ray. For once, Ray was driving his own truck. They did not head out of town, as Kev expected, instead they headed out to the lake.

"About time you learned how to shoot," Ray said.

The ground was muddy. It was a rare warm day in April. The afternoon sun was hot coming through the windshield. The tires were crunching over the end of the snow when Ray saw the moose from the dirt road. It stood looking at them. Ray wound down his window, and the moose just stayed there. Kev willed it to run, but it stayed and Ray reached back over the seat for his gun. It was already loaded. He shot the moose right from the truck, leaning out the driver's side window. The moose bellowed after the first shot and kept bellowing after it fell. Ray let off a few more shots and the sound stopped. They just left it there. Ray had no intention of going back and butchering the moose.

At the lake, Ray drank beer and set up the empty bottles on tree stumps and got Kev to aim at them. He gave Kev a beer to drink, and everything started to feel woolly. At first, Kev aimed carefully at the bottles, heeding Ray's instructions, bracing for kickback, lining up his shot, but after the beer, Kev wasn't so careful. He aimed at the ground and felt a pleasure at the sight of his bullets bouncing off it. He took the gun and ran around with it holding it in the air. Ray laughed and called him a wild man. Then Kev pointed the rifle at Ray, only for a second, but everything fell away from them. He lowered the gun and Ray had it off him in seconds. Kev didn't know his uncle could move so fast. Ray punched Kev hard in the guts.

"You never point a gun at me again. You understand me? You understand me?" Ray punched Kev again.

The next day after school, Kev hiked back to the place Ray had shot the moose. He stroked the moose's head, gently between the eyes, like he did with the ponies his nan's neighbours had. He kept visiting the spot over the summer and watched the moose's body bloat and fill with maggots as the weather got warmer. He saw when another animal pulled off one of the moose's legs. He heard the buzzing of flies, and observed the once-bloated body slowly deflate.

Kev got to know the woods that summer. There were places you could smell before you saw them. Hunters mounded up carcasses. Years of moose skins, rabbit guts and ptarmigan feathers all piled up together. There was one place, deep in the woods, that was different from the rest. When Kev first found it there was the usual stuff, moose hide, rabbit heads but he also found a whole dead fox flung up on top and four kittens.

Kev couldn't help going back to that place. It made him sick, but he couldn't stop himself from going to see what was added, a pet rabbit once, he knew it was a pet because it had big wide ears. He found more dead cats, one a friendly ginger one he knew from down the street and a beagle, called Misty, Kev had seen missing signs for.

One time he heard an ATV coming and he hid. He crawled deep into the overgrown alder scratching the shit out of himself and his chest soaking up mud from the wet boggy ground. He recognized Ray's footfall before he saw him. Kev felt his breath coming too quickly, he tried to keep quiet, something was crawling up his pants. It felt like a spider. Kev felt it creeping up his leg, but he lay still.

He didn't move. He wanted to get up and run. Kev kept his eyes almost closed, and watched from a slit between his eyelids.

When Ray came into view, he stopped and surveyed his cache. From where Kev lay, Ray seemed extra tall. Something caught Ray's attention at the ground by his feet, he crouched down and examined it. A bird started trilling a warning cry close by. Ray stood deliberately, he slowly took the gun from his back and slung it up on his shoulder, he turned in a slow circle and stopped with the gun pointed at the spot where Kev lay. Ray didn't say a word, but Kev was sure Ray knew he was there.

THE RED SHOES

~

The knocking on Kev's door sounded friendly. It wasn't the shotgun-rapid rap the cops used. Kev thought it might be some Jehovah's. Normal people knew better than to show up at his place without warning, even his mom. He slipped his shoes off and crept over to the door. Maybe the police were trying to trick him into a false sense of security with this gentle tappity-tap.

Kev cautiously looked out of his peephole and saw Evie. Her dark hair was in a ponytail. She was wearing a zip-up black hoodie and had her school bag slung over one shoulder. Her lips glistened with a fresh layer of clear gloss. He breathed in deep. Kev was awed that quiet little Evie had plucked up the courage to knock on his, Kev Babcock's, door at ten-thirty on a Thursday morning.

Evie looked like she was giving up on Kev answering. Kev thought for a moment of letting her walk away, but realized he longed to hear her voice. He opened the door, just as she was turning from it.

"Evie, what you doing here? Carter's not here. Were you looking for your brother?" Kev put some false shyness into his voice. "You come to see me?"

"Kev." Evie took a breath. He loved that she called him Kev, like his mom and his nan. Everyone else he knew called him Cocky.

"I was worried about Stevie, after last night," Evie said.

"Stevie? Stevie's fine, girl. Stevie's just grand. Don't be worried about him. I heard from him this morning already," Kev lied, and then regretted it. The chances of Stevie being up and communicative before noon were unlikely.

"You want to come in?" he asked Evie.

Evie hesitated; her eyes flickered over Kev's hand resting on the door frame. He gently beckoned her with his other hand.

"I've got to get back to school," she said. "They'll call Mom if I don't show up for math third period. I'm glad Stevie's okay."

"Stevie's like a rubber ball. Always bounces back. Come back some other time, but Evie, next time call first."

"Sure, Kev, sure." She was backing away, now less certain of him. Kev put his right hand up to shade his eyes and watched her leaving. He noticed the cat-shaped ears on her hoodie. He traced his finger over the heart-shaped tattoo underneath his right eye. He wanted to say something to soften his last words. He hadn't meant to sound so dismissive.

"Evie," he called out and she looked back. "Give me a smile," Kev said. The corner of Evie's lip curled up a little, but she turned away quick and kept walking.

~

Kev had heard stories of coyotes chewing their own legs off when they got caught in snares; Stevie had that look of a scared scavenger in his eyes yesterday. Couldn't sit still. Kev could remember him jerking around in his desk at school, always in trouble for getting out of his seat and fidgeting. One teacher, Miss Crocker, had made Stevie sit in a desk right next to hers at the front of the class. Sometimes she'd put his desk in a corner at the back, facing Stevie away from the rest of them.

Stevie had spent half his life running away from his dad, from Kev, from the cops. Maybe Kev should have made Stevie stick around a little longer last night. Stevie sure as hell didn't want to go to the hospital and Kev didn't need Stevie in a jangling state, quivering and talking too fast on the end of his couch all evening. Kev shook his head; he was acting soft. He had seen Stevie recover from more beatings, accidents, and humiliations than anyone else he knew. Kev tried to shake it out, the grit Evie had placed in his mind that was turning into a pearl of doubt. Stevie could be anywhere, sleeping off whatever he got up to after he left. Stevie was not Kev's responsibility, but Kev called Carter anyway.

"You seen Stevie around last night?"

"Nope," Carter replied, his voice still sleep laden.

"I wants to talk to him. Go find him."

"Now?"

"Fuck. Yes. Now."

An hour later, Carter called Kev back. "Mrs. Loder hasn't seen him since yesterday. His three-wheeler's not in the shed. She's not worried. Says he sometimes doesn't come home for a couple of days. Says if he owes us money, it's never anything to do with her."

"Keep looking."

"Why, Cocky, he steal something from your place?"

"Maybe," Kev said. The pearl of doubt had turned into a crab. A crab that was sitting in Kev's gut and was about to crawl back up his throat.

~

Carter checked for Stevie at Tyler McCarthy's house. Carter walked to The Drive In and picked up a burger, he checked at the parking lot of the arena, and up around the high school. Carter shot the shit with his mom at the Ultramar. He held the door open for customers and helped Brenda move some boxes around. He joked with the Doyle brothers, in to pick up their day's supply of beer.

"You seen Stevie around?" he finally asked his mom when the Doyles left.

"Not today. What you wants with him?"

"Nothing. Just, you know, business."

Brenda wrinkled her eyebrows, and then Dwayne came in to pay for his gas and Carter slipped out the door. Ashley Peddle was standing outside the Ultramar with her kid. She bummed a smoke from Carter and he stood outside with her. Ashley's kid's mouth was blue from the candy she was eating. It reminded Carter of Stevie's lips yesterday, before Evie had brought him back round.

Carter walked down to the fish plant. He was thinking about his sister, the way Kev was starting to look at Evie, he would have to have a talk with her. Tell her to stay the fuck away from Kev. Carter looked to see if Stevie's machine was parked down by the docks. His phone rang.

"Anything?" Kev asked him.

"No, b'y."

"Where the fuck is he?"

"When we were in high school, remember how Stevie had a reputation for liking to watch? People said he used to ride his bicycle around at night looking up at girls' bedrooms and shit like that?"

"More than a reputation, b'y. Found him hiding in the bedroom closet at that party."

"Fuck," Carter said as he remembered the look on Stevie's face when they had opened the closet door. "I heard he hangs out by the clearing, waiting for kids to go up there and start fooling around."

"Worth checking it, b'y, come get me. If he's not there, I'll just wait for him to turn up. His cousin has a cabin out on Salmonier Line. Stevie goes there to hide out sometimes."

Carter hardly rode his quad. He kept it in his mom's shed. He bought it with the first of the big money he made out West, but he didn't like riding as much as he thought he would. He didn't like being out in the woods. He always felt like someone was watching him, and he was never sure where he was; all the trees and rocks looked the same to him. Carter was a town man. He liked streets and houses and cars going by.

Carter only had one helmet, a full-face one that made his features invisible except for his eyes. He didn't have a helmet for Kev, but it didn't matter. The trail came right from Kev's place where Carter was picking him up. They bumped along. Carter was concentrating on driving the thing. The clearing was easy to get to from Kev's place and soon they were driving along the edge. Carter caught a flash of red up ahead. At first, his brain read the thing as a jerry can. He swerved off the trail to avoid it. The helmet made him feel like nothing was real, like he was wearing the glasses from his Xbox. Swerving past, he glanced down and his brain readjusted: not a jerry can, but a shoe. Stevie's red sneaker. Attached to Stevie's skinny leg. Kev swore, but Carter didn't hear him and Kev hardly heard himself. His voice sounded hollow in his own head; his unprotected ears fuzzy from the roar of the engine.

It took a few seconds for Carter to stop. He braked too fast and mud shot out from his wheels and kicked up onto Stevie who was lying on the ground behind them. They said nothing as they got off the machine and walked back over to him. Both of them stood over him in silence. There was no bringing Stevie back round this time. They both knew that.

"Poor fucking Stevie." Carter closed his eyes and made the sign of the cross. Kev did the same thing.

"What we gonna do?" Carter asked. He didn't like it, standing over Stevie.

"We could just leave him here. Someone will find him in the next couple of days." Kev was working out his options. He closed his eyes and lowered his head, then he looked up at the sky and opened his eyes.

"We've gotta hide him," Kev said. "Take off his shoes."

"Jesus, really, Cocky? What you want them for?"

"They stick out. Makes it too easy to spot him. And hurry the fuck up. We can't be hanging around here." It was mid-afternoon. They needed to move fast in case anyone came along.

Carter did what he was told. The dead weight of Stevie's leg was too real. Made it all too clear that Stevie wasn't alive. Carter shivered at the sensation as he held Stevie by his ankle and looked back hoping Kev would take over, but Kev just said, "Get on with it. The poor fucker."

Carter eased off the first shoe. The laces were undone, the tongue ripped on one side, it slipped off easily. The second shoe was on tighter. Carter had to grab hold of the heel with one hand. He had to put his thumb in the back of the shoe by Stevie's ankle and use it to pry the shoe off Stevie's foot. His thumb felt the dampness of Stevie's spongy sport sock, and then the shoe popped off like the red shell from a lobster claw leaving Stevie's tender foot vulnerable and childlike in his dirty white sock.

They carried Stevie, Carter at his head and Kev at his feet, off the trail. His head lolled around and his mouth opened. Carter felt himself panicking, counted to ten, and breathed out, like the priest taught him to in jail. They carried Stevie out of the clearing in amongst some close trees. Someone would have to crawl under the canopy of low-growing pines to find Stevie here. They covered him with dead leaves and a few branches.

"You can leave me here," Kev said. He was tying the strings of Stevie's shoes together. "Make sure you're out and about for the rest of today. Make sure people see you."

"Where you gonna be?" Carter asked Kev.

"I'm gonna deal with Stevie's machine, and then I'm taking Mom up to visit her auntie. And Carter, my son. You tell no one. No one. Ever."

Carter took off on his ATV. Kev looked down at Stevie's shoes in his hand. He had been unconsciously jiggling them up and down by the laces where they hung from one of his fingers. They were puppet-like, dancing around like they were alive. Kev shoved them up under his sweatshirt. He started up Stevie's ATV and tucked his sweatshirt into the front of his jeans to keep Stevie's shoes from slipping out. They felt oddly warm, and sometimes Kev had the sensation they were moving around, like instead of Stevie's runners he had a pair of kittens cuddled up to his belly.

Kev kept remembering things about Stevie he didn't want to. About Stevie as a little kid. About the time Stevie's shirt had slipped up and Kev had seen the bruises. About Stevie in high school, how he got caught hiding out in the showers of the girls' change room and said he was hiding from Kev, but it wasn't true. Kev had gone along with it at the time. He couldn't help feeling sorry for Stevie even though he was a perv. Kev remembered the time in grade nine when he'd chased Stevie down, and stolen his new shoes. They were just pieces of shit from the Walmart. Kev had thrown them up over the electrical lines behind the school. Stevie cried, and Kev felt sick afterwards, kind of like he did now. He actually went home and puked that day; he'd been young and didn't know how to regulate his emotions. When he had closed his eyes that night, he kept seeing Stevie walking down the street in his socks. The next day, Kev went to the school early and shoved a fifty-dollar bill into Stevie's locker. He saw Stevie find it and look around, like he was going to get caught at something.

Kev knew where he was going, towards a particular cliff edge, a place there was no gentle slope. No chance of the ATV getting stuck on a ledge. No chance of it getting caught on one of those brutalized pine trees that grew from rock straight out over the ocean, one half of it usually dead from salt spray and the other clinging to some semblance of life. In this spot, the machine would fall right down to the water. Kev drove the ATV close enough to the edge he got a twinge of vertigo. He got off the trike. He didn't hesitate, revved the engine good and pushed down on the handlebars. He wanted to leave tire tracks on the ground. He gave the thing a push and watched it go over, heard it bang against the side of the cliff as it went down and then a hiss when it hit the water.

He walked home along the trail, cradling the shoes tucked up in his shirt with one arm like they were trying to squirm away from him.

~

At the retirement home, Kev's great-aunt kept thinking he was her late husband, called him a slow-witted prick, and wanted to know where he'd been all this time. "I'm not James," Kev told her. She took out a tissue, spat generously on it, and tried to clean the tattoos off Kev's face.

That night, Kev walked along the old railway line to where it came up behind the school. Kids smoked there in Kev's day and a few still did. Three pairs of sneakers were already slung up over the power line and Kev flung Stevie's up. They caught the first time, the laces wrapping around the wires, then, as the shoes settled, they bounced up and down.

Kev met Carter at midnight. Kev had the keys to his Uncle Ray's truck. Ray used it to hunt and haul wood and it was already covered in scratches. Ray would either be passed out by now or staying at his girlfriend's house. They took a back road that butted up to the trail, parked the truck and walked in. It only took a few minutes to get to Stevie. Leaves clung to his face and clothes. Carter held him by his underarms and Kev took his feet. Not speaking, they carried him out. They lay Stevie on his back in the bed of the truck. They didn't have a tarp or a blanket. Kev decided this was less conspicuous. If they did get stopped, they could say they found Stevie out there and were bringing him home.

No other cars were on the road. They drove right by the RCMP station; it was closed up, empty for the night. There'd be a couple of cops out in a cruiser, but they could be anywhere in the region. They were probably parked up in the Tim Hortons parking lot in Bay Roberts waiting for something to happen. Kev headed towards the lake and killed the lights on the truck once they were on the dirt roads. He drove slowly, taking his time. There was enough moonlight that he could see the road and he carefully avoided bigger rocks and potholes, not wanting Stevie to get bruised up in the back. He didn't turn on the radio.

He had told Carter to leave his phone at home, and he'd left his too. That way there was no risk of any accidental GPS tracking or Carter trying to take a picture for future insurance. They drove around to the far side of the lake, and then Kev pulled the truck over.

It was a cool, windless night. They could smell the spot Kev was headed for before they saw it, the saccharine smell of death hanging in the night air. Anyone who came out here regularly would know this was the normal smell of this place. It was hunting season and lots of new carcasses would be lying around. They carried Stevie's body again, Carter tripped once on a root in the trail and they dropped him. Stevie's head bounced off the ground. They picked him back up and kept going. Carrying him around was starting to seem normal, like slinging corpses was part of their daily routine. They carried Stevie until they were at a mound of animal parts, then lowered him to the ground. There was a fresh moose head on top of the pile.

The moose's head had been sawn from its body. Its black wet eyes glistened in the moonlight. Carter went back to the truck for the shovel. Kev stood alone. He tried not to look too hard at what he was standing on. Places like this were all over the woods, places where hunters left hides, bones, and discarded body parts.

Kev made Carter lift the moose head down, then he tipped the loose top layers of the pile over. Carter began to shovel the remains of the pile to the side, then began to dig into the earth beneath. The first inches of ground were soft. Underneath that, the ground was hard.

Kev took a turn, sweat dripped down his face. He kept wiping away what felt like moose fur with the back of his hand. The smell was so thick, Carter said he was gonna puke but Kev told him he'd have to kill him if he did, and Carter wasn't sure if he was joking.

They were still digging when black sky tipped into early morning light. Kev finally said, "Enough," and they put Stevie in. They curled him into the fetal position. They both stood for a minute in silence, before covering Stevie first with dirt, and then, slowly piling layers of decaying entrails and skins back on top of it. A femur, a furred ear, the grim wetness of innards, and sinews of limbs unknown. Finally, the moose's lifeless head on top.

~

A few weeks later Kev was thinking about Evie, wondering if he called her if she'd go for a drive with him. He couldn't get her off his mind. He looked her up on Instagram. He was looking forward to seeing her pictures. He imagined it: Evie with her mom, Evie with Carter, Evie making duck lips, Evie from her bare shoulders up, pouting at the camera.

When Kev clicked on Evie's feed, her most recent picture wasn't a selfie at all but a picture of the power line behind the school, the sneakers hanging from it.

BANG, BANG, BANG

~

I felt the car pull up beside me. I was walking down Water Street, looking out over the water to Bay Mal Verde South. I would have ignored it in Toronto, but here I braced myself for a roadside inquisition: "Carly, you home for the wedding?" I expected, or "How's things up in Canada? Ha. Ha. Ha."

I kept walking but I turned my head. A tiny hand levelled a gun at me and pulled the trigger. I watched the gun get flipped up, cocked, and shot again, and the same thing once more. It was by the second shot, when I wasn't dead, that my brain picked up on the red plastic tip of the thing and I knew it was a toy. There wasn't the crack of a real bullet, just the child's voice saying, "Bang. Bang. Bang."

I never saw the face, I was busy staring down the gun, the practised flick of the hand and the small finger squeezing the trigger. As the car rounded the corner, the back window rolled back up. I didn't get the make of the car, only caught that it was beige, old, indistinct, like a calling card for rural poverty. It was a practised-perfect music-video drive-by.

This was a record year for shootings in Toronto, and even St. John's was having a spate of gun violence. I thought about the parents, one of them driving, probably laughing in the front seat. Probably mostly kids themselves, probably my brother's customers.

No one else was out on the street. No cars coming in either direction, no coffee shop to stumble into, no bus I could spontaneously board. No way to disappear fast out here except into the water or out to the woods. I felt like I had felt as a kid, as a teenager: stuck. Stuck in the middle of fucking nowhere with no conceivable escape. *This is not your life*, I reminded myself. I pictured my apartment in Cabbagetown, IKEA furniture and thrift-store finds; my office at the museum with my name on a plate by the door. A flat white on the way to work, lectures on preservation techniques for ancient textiles, or the protocol for repatriating artifacts. I longed for the noise of the city, the streetcar, but all I heard were the waves rushing at the shore.

When I got back to Joseph's place, I shut the door and leaned against it. I closed my eyes and saw the gun aimed at me. I was shaking. I made myself a cup of tea with sugar in it, the taste of nostalgia. It just made me feel lonely.

Joseph's house was a new build, a sprawling bungalow with big bay windows. Inside there were lots of hard beige tiles and large pieces of brown furniture. All the appliances were stainless steel. The house was backed onto the woods and removed from the main part of town. It looked down over the harbour and houses and, although the house was clean and modern, the yard was all *Dukes of Hazzard*. Joseph had inherited Finn's Disposals from our uncle, and his garbage trucks got parked up there at night, along with his SUV and two pickup trucks, one for hauling wood and the occasional load of trash when one of the compactors broke down, and the other his show piece: an impractical red gas guzzler on oversized wheels. He kept Finn's Disposals dumpsters up there too. There were two outbuildings with corrugated metal roofs and doors kept locked with heavy padlocks. And, of course, Joseph had his toys: the ATV, the snowmobile, the motorbike almost always shrouded in its body bag–like cover, and the dirt bike he bought for my nephew Joey. Joey hadn't ridden since he fell off and broke his arm and his mom threatened to go to the police since Joey was too young to be legally riding it. It was never exactly clear to me what they told the doctor at Emergency.

When Joseph came home, he brought Mary Brown's for our supper. He didn't notice I only ate the pickle off the top of my Big Mary and a couple of taters. We watched *RuPaul's Drag Race* together for a while, and guessed at who would win. Our one shared activity as teenagers had been TV-watching and we slipped into it comfortably, like in the old days when we shouted out answers to *Jeopardy!* or tried to guess the next plot twist on *Murder, She Wrote*.

After *RuPaul*, I went to bed. I was sleeping in my nephew's room. The bed was a child's bed in the shape of a race car, low to the ground and red. I had to curl my legs up. The light fixture had cars on it too, and around the top of the wall was a border of fire engines, constantly racing around the perimeter of the room in an infinite rush to an emergency they would never reach. Joey didn't come stay the night anymore. Joseph saw him every other weekend, at least for one meal. Joseph mostly just took him for breakfast: a quick drive through at the Tim Hortons for hot chocolate and donuts. The room remained ready with clean sheets. Joseph hadn't stored boxes of old tax receipts or his weight machine in it. Maybe he thought there might still be time for Joey to come stay. But Joey was too old and tall for that bed now.

I came out of the bathroom in the afternoon, with my hair curled, in a party dress I had bought on the internet. The dress was a rockabilly number, the kind of thing middle-aged women like me buy, trying to hold on to some vestige of cool without resorting to dyeing the grey streaks in our hair purple or navy blue. I was wearing it with Blundstones. Joseph said, "Nice shoes." What did he expect, I'd be teetering on a pair of hooker heels like Luanne's second marriage was a do-over of my high-school grad?

The only jacket I had was a bright blue North Face raincoat, and when I pulled it on over the dress Joseph said, "Wait, you look like a retard."

"Jesus Joseph, you can't be saying that."

"Come on, Carly. People will think you've had a breakdown or you've turned into a lesbian, or something."

He rifled through the front hall closet and pulled out his old leather jacket. I had always coveted that jacket and I pulled it on. It had that sexy supple feeling. I felt cool, like I was Patti Smith. I looked in the mirror,

"It's a bit aging rock star," I said.

"Better than looking like a—"

I put up my hand. "I'll wear it. Thanks."

I grabbed the things I needed from the pocket of my raincoat and shoved them into Joseph's jacket as I headed down the road. As I shoved a tampon towards the bottom of the pocket, I touched something hard with my fingers. I knew from the shape it was Joseph's old pocket knife. Our grandfather gave it to him: bone handled, with a sexy curve to its blade. I had been so jealous. All my presents got chosen by our nan and usually involved teddy bears, or were Nan's homemade projects, like a purse made of old jeans, or a crocheted dolly to cover up a spare toilet roll. The last time I'd seen the knife was in high school, we'd been at a bush party and Joseph had carved his and Luanne's initials deep in a tree. I'd yelled at him, told him the tree would die and he'd told me to stop being such a douche bag. I started angry crying and then ended up giving Dale Porter a hand job because he was nice to me.

It didn't take me long to walk downhill from Joseph's and hit Water Street. The wedding was at the United Church; they did divorcees. Every third car that drove by me honked, this time the greetings were friendly, most of the cars, like me, heading to the wedding.

In the church, I looked around. Took in everyone's faces, three years older than the last time I had seen them.

The reception was at the Loyal Orange Lodge, the LOL, on one of the streets in the "historic" part of town. I didn't get that drunk at first. I was well behaved. I danced to "Girls Just Want to Have Fun" with Luanne. I participated in the Loco-motion. Then there were so many people talking to me, emboldened by a few drinks they were asking me questions about my own life. I work at a museum, I'd say, and they'd smile imagining I sold tickets at the entrance, or maybe dressed up in old-timey outfits and showed people around, and I didn't disabuse them of this idea. Mostly people wanted to tell me how many kids they had, about jobs they had gotten, houses they had bought, parents in hospital, parents back from hospital, parents dead. Then there was the gossip too. Whose son was in jail, just back from jail, husband had left her, couldn't have a baby, miscarried, wasn't speaking to her sister, who was laid off, let down, lying low. A lot of diabetes and IVF were going on. No one asked me about Joseph, they all knew how he was doing with his big house on the hill, his suits, and the rumours about where his money really came from.

When Luanne and her new husband left the reception, Luanne threw her bouquet at me and I caught it on reflex. Of course, I caught it. I switched from the champagne and got serious at the bar with Luanne's Uncle Mort (the gay one) and some whisky. Mort was only a few years older than me, but I still called him Uncle Mort. He lived in Montreal and joked how, there, he insisted on being called Mortimer, as Mort does not do well on bilingual dating sites. Then Mort and I were the only ones left at the bar. A few drunk stragglers were on the dance floor and the bartender was pointedly wiping down tables.

I hugged Mort goodbye. His mother lived just down the street and he stumbled out the front door to head to her house. I went for a last pee. The whisky hit me as I stood watching my swaying, red-faced reflection in the bathroom mirror and contemplated the walk uphill to the comfort of my nephew's car-shaped bed. The booze, the flight from Ontario, the general exhaustion of being in my hometown had caught up with me and I needed sleep. By the time I emerged from the bathroom, the last of the dancers were heading out the front door and I was the only guest left inside. A party would be continuing on somewhere, but no one had invited me.

The parking lot behind the LOL was famous for a murder. I was related to the murdered girl, Mary Catherine Finn. On September 4, 1824, she had been raped and killed in the back alley that used to be where the parking lot was now. Dad had told me this story with glee. Mary Catherine's death was famous, and he liked to crow about his connection to her, like her death was a sideshow act that made him look cool. He bragged about it the way the teenage boys I grew up with bragged about watching snuff films. There were ghost stories about Mary Catherine; Luanne and I had come here a few times at night looking for her, and once freaked ourselves out so much I'd peed my pants.

I could hear noise out in the parking lot. I thought I'd just go check. Maybe someone would be sober, or sober enough, to give me a ride home. I could check for an Uber, I thought to myself, and was laughing at this thought as I headed out the door. You still had to order cabs twenty-four hours ahead out here. I stumbled on the stairs as I was coming down them.

Only one car was in the parking lot, and about eight people, and when their faces turned to stare at me coming out of the building, I realized they were all young. In that odd space between teenager and adult. Maybe the oldest was twenty. Twenty years ago, Luanne and I would have been part of this crowd. They all looked familiar,

I could have guessed at half of their last names, but I didn't know them, and they did not know me, and they were not welcoming of a stranger. They glared, the wide-eyed stare they used around here to stake territory, then they ignored me. I was an adult, but a lone one and female, I was no threat to the bottles they were drinking from. The smell of teenagers assaulted me: smoke, cheap alcohol, skunky pot, body spray. I was ready to go, preparing myself for the slow march back to Joseph's, the sobering cool air. One of the boats was in, and I could hear the thrum of its engine down by the cold storage. I was walking away when the fight started. I heard the noise of anger and I turned to look, despite myself.

He was one of those boys. Gym hard, whitened teeth, drunk and something more, although I couldn't put my finger on it. He was yelling at a girl, getting in close to her with his face, his hands clenched into fists. He grabbed her by the shoulders. "Mandy, why do you always do this to me?" He was sobbing, and it was like the small crowd was forgiving him his casual violence because of the tears pouring down his face. They were lit by the lights of the parking lot, and it was eerily theatrical.

"You're a fucking piece of shit, Tyler," she yelled at him.

"Mandy, you're a fucking whore," he shouted through his tears. His hand gripped the upper arm of the girl and was squeezing tight. Mandy was one of those girls without body fat. She was wearing a puffy winter jacket but it hung over a cropped white sweater and her pierced navel was exposed to the cold air. She was shrinking her head into her jacket trying to get warm even as she tried to pull away.

One of the other girls in the small group yelled, "Let go of her, Tyler, you're hurting her."

"Mind your own business, Evie. This is between them," another girl said, like she didn't want the spectacle interrupted.

"Fuck off, Tyra," Evie said.

"Fuck you, Evie."

Evie kept looking towards me, where I had turned at the edge of the lot, like she thought I could fix this. Like it was the schoolyard, and somehow, I was expected to play teacher. Tyler gave Mandy a vicious shake.

I avoided, whenever I could, being an authority figure. I had at least twenty years and two university degrees on top of this crowd. Evie looked at me again, waiting for me to act.

I started to walk over to Mandy and Tyler. When I was about five feet away, Tyra pushed another boy out in front of me.

"Get her to mind her own business, Cody," she said.

His jeans were dirty and his thin lip twitched slightly. He was giving me a fuck-off-outta-here stare. I was trying to remember if 911 worked in this part of Newfoundland yet. It never used to, I used to know the number for the volunteer fire department, I was trying to recall it. I wasn't entirely sure I had cell reception.

I ignored the boy, and yelled, "Let go of her" at Tyler, the words sounding ineffectual as they left my mouth.

"Mind your own business, missus," the boy, Cody, said.

"Leave her, Tyler," Evie called out. I heard Mandy whimper.

"He can't be shaking her like that," I said to Cody, and I went to walk past him. He pushed me and I stumbled back and fell sideways, I caught myself with one hand on the ground. Some instinct I left behind a long time ago came back. Something kicked in and I sprang up fast.

Cody had turned away from me after I fell and part of me suspected he was ashamed. I grabbed Cody by the shoulder and swung him around. I looked him straight in the eye, put my face right up to his. My voice changed, my smoothed-out mainland accent went all Bay and any quiver that had been in my voice earlier was gone. I moved my head, gave it a little shake, and put some swagger in my movement before I let the words out, right in his face.

"Do you know who I am, b'y? Do you know who I am?" His hands were at his sides and I could see the hesitation, but he was thinking of raising them. I spit the last words at him. "I'm Joseph Finn's fucking sister."

I glanced over for just a moment. Tyler had let go of Mandy and all eyes were on me and Cody, seeing if he had it in him to take things further, seeing if he was tough enough, bad enough to hit a woman, a woman who claimed she was Joseph's sister. I reached in my pocket then, thought I'd pull out my phone and call the cops.

Or at least try to. What came out was the knife, and without thinking I flicked it open.

"Shit," I heard one of the previously silent bystanders exhale. I looked at the knife in my hand, vicious and sharp. I saw fear in Cody's eyes. I felt the power I had, that I could hurt him if I wanted to. Then I glanced around in time to see Mandy, now free, turn and raise her skinny arm. She punched Tyler square in the middle of his face. Blood and tears streamed down his nose.

"I'm calling the cops," I said.

"I already did," said Evie.

I was still holding the knife between me and Cody, I heard ragged breathing, like a sick animal. The breathing was coming from me.

"Come on, Tyler," I heard Mandy say, and she was guiding him, sobbing and holding his bleeding nose, to the car. Tyler kept saying, "I'm sorry, baby. I'm so sorry." A couple of other kids got in with them and the car doors were slamming, the engine starting up.

Cody backed away from me.

"Crazy bitch," he said and started running and I heard the sirens.

I stood for a moment looking at the knife, looking around at the remaining kids staring at me and the car pulling out fast, until the Evie girl yelled at me, "Run. Fucking run." And we all ran, me and these kids heading down the lanes we knew the cop car could not go.

When I got to Joseph's, he was sitting in a rocker, the rocker that Luanne bought from an antique store in St. John's when she was pregnant. He was dressed for a business meeting in a suit and tie, but he was rocking back and forth with a shotgun on his lap.

"Jesus Christ, Joseph!" I was thinking suicide, until he looked accusingly at me.

"How'd you get home?"

"I walked," I said. But I'd run, and I was out of breath and I knew I looked like I'd been fucking someone's husband in the janitor's closet of the hall.

"Go to bed out of it," he said.

"Joseph? I'm an adult, remember? Don't tell me what to do."

"Go to bed and lock the bedroom door and don't open it, no matter what happens. Don't open it for anyone."

I didn't argue, and I allowed myself to notice that the lock on the bedroom door was a dead bolt and there were bars on the window. Of course, I'd noticed before, I just pretended to myself that things were different. Like Joseph didn't have video-surveillance cameras set up all over the place and a baseball bat stuck in an umbrella stand by the front door. No one in our family ever played baseball.

I took off my party dress and pulled on a T-shirt. Then I put the jacket back on and pulled it tight around me and lay in bed listening. Joseph had the TV on, too low for me to make out words. Eventually, I heard the front door open and shut again. It was past late and into the early morning by then. Far in the distance I heard gunshots. A shotgun, ringing out. Bang. Bang. Bang. Once, twice, three times and I pulled the covers over my head. The sun was coming up, and I thought I'd just wait it out until morning. I woke up smelling bacon, hearing gunshots again.

I packed my suitcase, tucking Joseph's jacket in the bottom and stashing the knife with it. When I came out of the bedroom, the table was set. A pitcher of orange juice, a glass already poured at my place. Joseph was frying breakfast and Joey was shooting people on the TV screen.

SKEETER

~

Since lockdown, Kev has been busy dispatching deliveries. Knock, stand back, wait for payment to be handed over, then he puts the package down.

It's a lot of work and not the kind he likes. He doesn't usually deal directly with the customers, but his workforce is down. He used to have Carter and Stevie and a couple of other b'ys he could count on.

Carter got caught for some dumb-ass shit: cabin break-ins. Kev had gone to the cabins with him, but fuck, what was Carter thinking putting those generators for sale on Kijiji? He was out now, but part of his release order was to stay away from Kev. They send messages back and forth on Carter's kid sister Evie's Facebook account, she never uses it anymore. Carter sends videos of dogs surfing and Kev responds with various laughing emojis.

Kev is just glad Carter wasn't inside when the pandemic started. The prison in St. John's is a nightmare, Kev knows. Flu, cold, lice, they get you however careful you are. This virus could get in there and wipe the whole prison population out.

Kev tried out a couple of other b'ys to be on his crew, but not everyone is cut out for this kind of work. He's taken on a couple of young ones. They're all still underage, if they get caught, they won't be charged as adults, but he's not sure how reliable they are. They're tough enough, but are they loyal? Kev's not too worried, the cops don't give a shit right now about Kev's business. They all know he is performing a public service, getting what little product he can get in, to his customers. Giving everyone a little relief and stopping shit from boiling over in homes where people are stuck together all day.

The supply chain is fucked by travel regulations. Kev's boss Joseph says they'll figure it out. No one is working, even the court appearances are getting delayed and demand for product is up and supply is down. They're limiting purchases, just like the grocery store where it's two loaves of bread and only one chicken at a time. When the weather gets better, it will be easier to get boats in, maybe even a private plane. "Times like this you got to take risks, show what you're made of. Can't roll over in the face of adversity," that's what Joseph says. Kev and him have seen more of each other lately. They both live alone, so they take a little social time after business. They sit on lawn chairs in Joseph's garage keeping the door open.

Kev always has something legal to drop off in his truck when he is out and about. He goes shopping for his mom, he doesn't want her going into stores and exposing herself to risk. He drops off care packages at other houses too. Feels like it's the right thing to keep his eye on his crowd. Before heading to his mom's, he heads to Carter's mom's place. He drops off some toilet paper and yeast. Brenda laughs at the toilet paper,

"I'm well stocked, Kev, we get first dibs at the store when the order comes in, but I'll take it anyways, never know when there'll be another shortage." But she's pleased with the yeast. They talk for a while from a distance. Brenda says Carter's doing alright. Working for Finn's Disposals.

Kev's always looked after Carter and his people. They grew up together. He was going to send Carter's mom and Evie away on a vacation this spring. Kev imagined them hanging out on the beach in Cuba. Kev wanted to reward Carter for his loyalty. Carter knew a lot of stuff Kev wished he didn't. A package holiday for his family was a good insurance policy. Kev even daydreamed about showing up and surprising them. Finding Evie lying by the beach. He'd take her out on a Jet Ski. Evie didn't come to the door to see Kev when he dropped by, although he knew she was home. Brenda said she was in the shower, but her hand tapped the door frame when she said this and Kev didn't believe her. Evie is shy, that's part of what Kev likes about her.

"You need anything, let me know," Kev says to Brenda, and he means it.

That vacation would have been good for Evie, helped her come out of her shell. And Kev could have got it cheap; Dan, who owned the travel agency, he owed Kev big time for sorting out that trouble his daughter was in. Rich guys never knew how to solve their own problems. Just look at all those politicians up at Confederation Building, paying off their kids' drug debts with prepaid credit cards. Fools, if buddy knows he can get money from you, he'll come back time and time again. And those politicians, all of them have secrets they don't want getting out. Easy picking for extortion. But Kev's not into that. Feels dirty to him.

Kev accepted a couple of cases of baby formula and some boxes of diapers from Brian Peddle. Usually, he wouldn't fuck around with this barter shit, but it was difficult times and Kev knew he had to cut some of his regular customers some slack. His boy Terrence's girlfriend had a baby in March and Kev is driving the stuff over to her place. He hasn't been able to throw Terrence any work since he froze on a job. Just didn't get out of the car when Kev needed him to man up and help him shake down that fucker from town council who didn't vote how he was supposed to. Wouldn't have had that problem with the young ones he's taken on, Cody, or his girl Tyra. He'd heard Tyra gave one of the older McCarthy kids a bloody nose. Rammed her palm into his face in some self-defence move she'd seen online after he called her friend Braydon a fag. Kev heard all sorts of things, but this had the ring of truth to it.

He's headed to Terrence's the first time he sees the dog. He's driving down the street and the dog rushes out right in front of Kev's truck. He hits the brakes hard. He stops inches from it. The dog is stood in the middle of the road staring at him. It's a fucking beauty. A king of a dog, it cocks its head at Kev and Kev nods his head at it. The dog is wagging its tail, although it is still barking.

He hears someone calling, "Here, you stupid shit, here!"

Justin. Kev didn't know he was back, thought he was out West for good. Kev takes in the house, used to be Justin's uncle's, there are dead plants in the window, brown leaves stuck against the glass. Can't be Justin who grew those, looks like he had a woman, and surprise, surprise, she's gone. The place looks like a fucking wrecking yard. Beat-up cars and a shitload of machines. There are half-rusted-out ATVs, a dune buggy, and an Argo with a BBQ tied on to the back. Christ, if this was on his mom's street, she'd be losing her shit. Kev wouldn't stand for it. He doesn't understand why no one's told Justin to clean his property up.

It must be because most of the neighbours are old.

The dog had drifted into Justin's neighbour's yard, it was crouching right in the centre of their lawn. Kev rolled down his window, "Justin, you gonna pick up your dog's shit, son?"

Justin looked up. "What shit? I don't see no shit."

"He just took a dump on your neighbour's lawn. And you know I almost hit him. Needs to be on a leash, b'y, or you need to learn how to keep him under control."

"Why don't you mind your own fucking business, Kevin?"

Kev stared. Who the fuck did Justin think he was? He always did take things too far, even when they were kids.

Justin spat on the ground. He had a wrench in his hand. A couple of cars had pulled up behind Kev, the one at the back, must not have known it was Kev's truck blocking traffic, started honking. Kev moved on, but he gave Justin a hard stare, and yelled out, "I'll be seeing you, Justin. I'll be seeing you real soon."

He wasn't sure if he meant the threat or not. But fuck man, he had been so close to killing that dog, that dog was fucking majestic and a goofy fucker like Justin didn't deserve him.

~

Kev can't get that dog out of his mind. How close he'd been to hitting it. It pisses him off. Justin was one of those guys that got good stuff then fucked it up. He must have inherited that house, and he was letting it fall the fuck apart. And that dog, who the fuck sold Justin a dog? No one round here would trust Justin with so much as a ferret. Couldn't be someone local.

Kev's dropping off stuff at his mom's, he's pretty sure it's nothing she needs urgently, she's just lonely.

"I need a can of peas, and some carrots. And I'd die for a KitKat."

He'd brought her two Aero bars yesterday.

He FaceTimes her at least once a day, but she likes to see him in the flesh. He got her a box of medical masks and he makes her wear one even when they're talking outside, although she pulls it down under her mouth every time she speaks.

In his line of work sometimes you have to get in close to people and he doesn't want his mom getting sick from him.

Kev puts three bags down on his mom's step, knocks on the door then backs off. Shirley opens her door and lets Panda out on a long retractable lead. Panda hurries over on her short legs to Kev and then flops on her back expecting a belly rub, which Kev gives her. Kev asks his mom about Justin, and Shirley pulls her mask down.

"Kevin, I thought I told you. Justin Hillier moved back a year ago, and Laura and her son Parker moved in with him. They were engaged. I seen pictures of Laura's ring. The Haywards, next door, well, he was already in bad shape. They were real close with Justin's uncle, but Justin didn't do nothing for them. Didn't even shovel a path to their front door in the winter. And there was always a racket. I heard he punched a hole right through the wall into the Haywards' living room, knocked a photograph of their daughter's wedding right off the wall. Mr. Hayward was on his way round to have a talk with Justin when he had the stroke. He's still up in rehab, and Mrs. Hayward went to stay with the daughter. The family can't even visit him in hospital. It's a sin."

"What about Laura?"

"I seen on Facebook she's back living with Parker's dad. Why you so interested? Laura's trouble, don't be getting involved with that."

"Use those wipes I got you before you put your stuff away."

"I know, I know. Can you get me more of those? Bernie says everywhere is out of them, and I said I'd ask you."

"Loves you, Mom." Kev is walking away.

"Kev?"

"I'll try and get some more wipes. Stay safe!"

Next he drops off a bag of stuff at Arlene Loder's. He's tucked a discreet bottle of Golden Wedding whisky in her bag along with some cans of milk, soup, stew and some hand sanitizer. He hopes she doesn't drink the sanitizer. He got a line on a couple of boxes of purse-sized bottles. He hands them out to everyone. It dries the shit out of his skin, but he still uses it. He's constantly rubbing in moisturizer to stop his hands from getting sore. He accidently got one that was lavender scented and the smell reminds him of the old-age home. His auntie's locked in up there, and he feels for her. That place is grim, and she'll miss her visitors and the odd push around the grounds.

He has some blue latex gloves in the truck, in case Joseph needs him to do something dirty, but they've been trying to keep business as clean as they can. There's enough risk in it without getting a fucking disease. And the sooner it's over, the better. For one thing, he's tired of reassuring his mom it's not the end times. He thinks she kind of enjoys it, living at a time she calls the end of the world. This way nothing will happen after she's gone, and she won't miss out on any gossip because everyone will be dead with her.

He cruises past Justin's on his way home. No sign of him, but he sees the dog. It's chained up in the backyard. No doghouse, its water dish is knocked over. Kev parks outside. There's dog shit all over the Haywards' front yard.

The dog stands up when Kev approaches, its ears are pointing up and it's panting. Kev wonders how long it has been there with no water. He's got a case of water in the back of the truck. Keeps it around in case they get a boil-water order and his mom freaks out.

The dog doesn't bark when he approaches. It's real quiet. Kev talks to it low.

"Hey, big man, you thirsty?"

It watches, but doesn't lunge forward at him. Kev cautiously flips the empty dish over with his foot. He doesn't crouch, he's not sure if the dog gets him yet. He pours the water in the dish standing up. And the dog doesn't drink until Kev is backing away. It drinks half the water then sits down. It gazes up at Kev.

"Sorry, buddy, I got nothing to feed ya."

Kev knocks on Justin's side door, there's no answer. He tries the handle, but it's locked. He peers in the window. Kev shakes his head, the dog whines. Kev goes round the back, there's a pair of old boots by the back door, Kev sticks his hand inside and pulls out a key. He unlocks Justin's door and calls out. He steps inside. The place is filthy. The living room contains outdated pastel furniture that must have been Justin's uncle's, a rug hook of a caribou on the wall, the dead plants and a plastic kids' slide that must be left over from Laura. Then there is Justin's stuff: video games, engine parts on the coffee table. A box of ammo, just lying there. No wonder his woman left. In the kitchen there are beer bottles full of cigarette butts, a dirty dog bowl on the floor, it looks like Justin never cleans it out.

Kev pauses, listens, then calls out again. "Justin, you home?" He walks up the stairs, and looks in at Justin's unmade bed. He notices the linen closet door at the end of the hallway is slightly ajar, he walks towards it slowly, half expects Justin to jump out with a gun. He grabs the door fast and pulls it open. A box falls from the top and hits him on the head. The closet is stuffed with fireworks. Boxes and boxes of one of those collections you buy in the summer or for New Year's. Devil's Works, the kit is called. A picture of a red-horned devil with fireworks exploding from his mouth on the side of the box. Kev remembers, the cops coming around, over a year ago, asking him questions about stolen fireworks. Kev shook his head. Justin was so stupid. How did he think he was gonna get rid of the things? Kev put the box that had fallen on his head back. Pushed the closet door back to how it had been. He went back into Justin's room on a hunch, opened the door to his bedroom closet. They were stacked in there too. And Justin had been smoking in this room, not two feet away from the closet there was an ashtray set on a chair he was using as a bedside table. Kev shakes his head and goes back down to the kitchen and opens a cupboard, there is a bag of cheap dog food. He puts food in the dog dish, and brings it outside and gives it to the dog. He puts Justin's key back in the boot.

In his truck, Kev squeezes out hand sanitizer, it stings as he rubs it in.

~

Kev drives by Justin's house every few days. If Justin's home the dog is out nosing around the wrecks on his lawn. He sees the dog chase right across the road after that running chick. She stops and stands still and the dog leaps up around her, barking its head off. It doesn't make contact but she looks terrified. Justin calls the dog back and it goes to him, but not straight away. Justin doesn't say anything to the woman, and she doesn't even turn to look at him. Kev has pulled over to watch. Justin can't see him. Kev winds down his window. "You okay?" he asks when the running chick gets level with him.

"Yeah, thanks." She nods but she doesn't look it.

Kev asks around. Turns out the whole neighbourhood is terrified of the dog. School kids walk around the next block to avoid going down their own street.

The woman across the road won't let her grandkids play in the front yard when they come over.

"Justin's got them all scared shitless. Threatened to kill the cat that belongs to missus across the street if she went to town council. At least that's what I heard," Brenda tells him when he stops in the Ultramar for gas and gossip.

Kev is heading out of his house on Tuesday afternoon when he hears gunshots coming from up behind his house, up in the hills by the clearing. Probably some moron shooting skeets, but it is way too close to town to be at that. He wonders if it's Cody. It's the kind of thing he might do. He wonders if Cody has still got product on him. It would be just like that kid to get distracted and head up there with one of his fucking uncles. The fucking McCarthy boys were always trouble. He'll have to go up there, knock some sense in their heads. Kev doesn't have his own machine, usually borrows Carter's, but this time he decides he'll walk up. Get those b'ys gone before the police come calling. He doesn't want the cops up there sniffing around. Not that he thinks they'd find anything, but you never know. Some of them that get stationed out here turn into cowboys, think they can build careers by digging around in stuff best left in the past.

There's a pause in the shooting, but Kev can hear the rumble of male voices. Another round of shots ring out, those b'ys are way too close to town. A bullet could go through some nan's window for fuck's sake, and they aren't even that far from the school.

"Hey!" Kev yells. His voice is loud and low. "That you, Cody? That you, b'y, that you causin' this racket?"

It comes at him like an avalanche, the dog is all motion and speed. It looks wild, it's frothing at the mouth and hurtling towards him. He hears ringing through the trees, the unmistakable sound of a smoker's cough. Kev kneels down just before the dog gets to him. He holds out his hand palm up and low. The dog crashes into him then starts whimpering. Kev is on the ground, the wind knocked right out of him and the dog is burying its big head into his chest. Kev strokes the head, sees a piece of the dog's ear is missing. He catches his breath and sits up. When he rubs the dog down, he sees its hind leg is bleeding too.

"Those fuckers."

"Come, dog. Get back here," he hears Justin call.

Kev scratches the dog's head. The dog does not return to Justin.

~

The vet doesn't ask Kev too many questions. They went to school together, him and Samantha. He tells her he found the dog in the woods and that he wants to keep him, all of which is true. She knows Kev is good to dogs. He cried like a baby when they put Whiskey down. The vet comes out of the building herself to get Kev's payment. He slips her a little package and she looks relieved. It's harder than usual, Kev suspects, to skim a little from a legitimate stock of pharmaceuticals. They have a long-standing arrangement, whenever he's got to bring Panda in for his mom, he brings a little something, and Dr. Pike always gets him a good discount.

"You're looking good, girl," he tells her, but she looks worn out and she has three inches of brown hair coming in at her roots.

The dog sits in the passenger seat of Kev's truck, it rests its heavy head right on his shoulder as he drives, and even though it's drooling a bit, Kev lets it keep its head there.

Kev doesn't hide the dog. He takes it everywhere. It rides up in the front of his truck. It waits patiently beside him, staring up at him with longing, wanting his attention, while he conducts his business in secluded driveways and around the back of warehouses. He takes it to meet his mom, and Panda goes nuts when she sees it in Kev's passenger seat, baring her teeth and dancing up on her hind legs as she barks. The dog stays quiet, and Kev rewards it with a chicken wiener. At home the dog sits at his feet when he watches TV, it sleeps stretched out on the bed next to him and Kev wakes to find its paw draped over him. He's got the dog on good food now, he's ordered frozen meals for it from the internet, and the dog's coat is shiny. Its eyes all cleared up from where they used to be bloodshot.

Kev hears that Justin is talking shit about him, telling everyone he's going to make Kev pay.

It's about a month since he picked up the dog when Justin comes knocking on Kev's door at 3 a.m. He's slurring, must be fucking loaded. He's come on a dune buggy, part of his backyard collection, and it is parked in the middle of the road with the lights and engine still running. Kev can hear Justin at the door, banging away. "You stole my fucking dog, you asshole, I want it back. You think you're tough, Kev, come show me. We'll see who the big man is." The dog, Kev named him Skeeter, doesn't make a sound. "Good boy, Skeety b'y. Go lie down," Kev says. The dog retreats to the bedroom.

Kev opens his door.

"Gimme my fucking dog back." Justin staggers back a bit.

"Not your dog, Justin."

"It's my dog and you know it."

"You know what they says, b'y. Finders keepers. And you're no good at keeping much from what I hear."

"I'll call the cops."

Kev laughs. "Go right ahead then." He cracks his neck, pulls his shoulders up, lets Justin see just how built he is. Justin backs off. Takes off on the dune buggy and knocks over Kev's neighbour's garbage bins. Kev cleans it up. He doesn't need this hassle. He knows everyone is behind their curtains watching. He sees old Mrs. Thorne's curtain twitch so he waves, she opens it up and waves back. He'll bring her some squares soon, his mom always said Mrs. Thorne was good to her when she went through hard times. Helped get her that job at the store, before it closed up and moved to Carbonear. She'd liked her job working the lotto counter. She got to gossip all day and she cashed all the government cheques, knew who was getting how much for what.

~

His mom is the one who tells him Mr. Hayward died. All alone. His wife hadn't seen him in weeks.

Kev can't imagine his mom being in a hospital bed and him not being able to visit. He remembers what it was like when his sister died. Long days in the hospital, his mom yelling at doctors, crying, the priest holding her hand. He remembers Annabelle's white coffin, his mom burying her with her favourite pink poodle toy, and Kev had tucked in his own favourite toy, a fire engine he called Ernie. Him and his mom never talk about Annabelle, although he knows his mom keeps a picture of her beside her bed.

He hasn't heard from Justin, but someone has scratched the side of his truck with a set of keys and he can't think who else would be at that. He drives by Justin's place, it looks even worse than before, the junk in Justin's yard has spread and is slowly encroaching on the Haywards' side. He hears from his mom that Mrs. Hayward is distraught. Her daughter's place is overcrowded, she's sharing a room with her grandson. Doesn't want to come home and live by herself, but she can't afford a place in the retirement village close to her daughter if she can't sell the house. And who's going to buy the place with Justin living in the house next door with his stuff spreading like mould all over the yard?

"You know if the Haywards have insurance?"

"I'll find out for you, son."

"Don't tell them I'm the one that asked."

Shirley nods.

DROWNING

~

Ryan feels the dirt and sweat collecting in all the crevices of his body. Inside his elbows, his armpits, his crotch. The corners of his mouth are gunged up with a grey paste of dust, spittle and sweat. The heat is making the garbage stink. Carter and Ray are smoking more than usual to try and cover up the smell, but the smoke and the fumes of rot are hitting Ryan and giving him waves of nausea. When he gets close to Carter, beneath the smoke, he can smell Carter's acidic sweat, sharp with an edge of whatever deodorant he uses. Something scented, with a name like Phoenix or Valiance. Ray, if Ryan accidently gets too close to him, has deep offensive body odour. Ray's funk is of unwashed clothes, alcoholism, and despair.

They are towards the end of their shift and Ray is even moodier than usual. He keeps yelling at them to hurry up.

Ryan's hands are itching inside his gloves. Ryan and Carter are both on edge. Ray is jerking the garbage truck around turns like he wants them to fall off from where they hang on to the back of the vehicle.

"Fuck's sake, Ray. You trying to kill us?" Carter yells up to him.

"Don't be swearing on me. If I was trying to kill you, you'd know it."

Ryan can tell by how Carter keeps his eyes closed, he is doing an anger-management breathing exercise. Ryan's shrink got him to do similar things, but not for his anger, to manage what she referred to as his invasive thoughts. Ryan has a vivid image of Carter being thrown from the back of the truck, his skull splitting as it hits the concrete curb. He shakes his head, trying to get rid of this vision. When he brings his water bottle to his lips, he can smell garbage on his hands. He worries about finding a baby in the back of the truck. He pictures a baby lying on top of black garbage bags. It isn't dead, it opens its eyes. Then he pictures the compactor starting up, smashing its contents together. He made the mistake of googling "stuff found by garbagemen" a few weeks ago. Now he gives every bag three firm shakes and listens before sending it into the back of the truck. He is horrified at the idea of sending a living thing into the chomping mouth of the compactor. He worries about babies, puppies, kittens, even rats.

They stop at a pile of bags, a collection from three houses Ryan had gathered while Carter cleared the other side of the road, both he and Carter start throwing the bags in, when one of them slips from Carter's hand and splits open.

"Fuck." They throw the rest in then look at the mess they have made. Used tissues, a beige Band-Aid, onion peels, and a human toe. Carter nudges the toe with his boot and it rolls away. One of the ballsy seagulls that has been pestering them all day swoops in and grabs it. Carter and Ryan look at each other, and watch the seagull fly away with its treasure, its companions squawk and flap about it jealously.

"Baby carrot," says Carter, but they both knew it wasn't.

When Ryan gets home his mom and nan are sitting in the kitchen drinking tea, he can tell by the silence as he enters that they have been talking about him.

"Ryan? How was work? Come join us, after you've had a shower," his mom says.

He wants to scream, and swallowing down the emotions he feels, his eyes tear up.

"Ryan? Sweetheart?" his mom says.

He has to get out of this house. He goes upstairs and grabs clothes and a towel, "I'm going for a swim," he says.

"Alone?" But he is out the door. It takes him a while to walk out to the lake. He doesn't swim right off the dock where people could see him, but fights his way down an old trail, to a spot his dad used to take him. They haven't been swimming together for years.

Ryan strips off and doesn't try to pull his swim trunks onto his sweaty body. The water is cold, painful even, but he welcomes it. He makes his way in, slipping on the rocky bottom. When he is up to his waist, a wave comes, and he loses his footing and he is in. The shock of the cold causes him to make a stupid high-pitched whooping sound. Girlish, he thinks, although he knows this is sexist. He feels embarrassed, then makes the sound again with intention. He splashes up a storm hammering his arms on the surface of the lake. He dunks his head under and scrubs his hair. He does a furious front crawl out into the lake and this warms him up. Then he floats on his back, riding up and down on the waves and staring up at the clouds and blue sky, for the first time in a long time, his brain is empty. He just feels the cold of the water and sees the sky.

~

The next day, they are outside Arlene Loder's house and her door is wide open. This is unusual.

They take her stuff from an old oil tank that's been converted into a garbage container, a door cut from the top and a handle welded on. The bags are just small kitchen bags, and they aren't supposed to take these, but they do. Bottles clink as they throw them.

Ray is pulling out, but Carter hesitates and looks towards Arlene's door. Then he walks over towards it and Ryan, despite himself, follows. Carter stops on the threshold and calls in the through the open door, "Arlene, you alright, my love?"

They hear a sound, a rattle coming from inside. Carter steps inside and Ryan follows. A door from the front hallway is open into the living room. Arlene is lying on the floor, asleep and snoring loudly. An empty whisky bottle beside her. She's wearing a ratty robe pulled over a thin nightdress and one of her breasts has slipped out. Carter steps over, takes a blanket made from yellow-and-cream crocheted squares from the couch, and covers Arlene with it. He gently turns her onto her side into the recovery position. He takes the whisky bottle into the kitchen. Ryan follows, finds a glass, and fills it with water and places it beside Arlene. They leave, shutting the door behind them.

When they finish for the day, Ryan doesn't start walking towards home but turns in the other direction.

"Where you going?" Carter calls after him.

Ryan wants to lie, but can't think anything up. "The lake," he says.

"How come?" says Carter.

"Going for a swim."

"I'll come with you," Carter says and jogs towards Ryan and walks beside him.

There's a couple of families swimming from the dock. Kids wearing inflatable water wings and fooling around with pool noodles. A big yellow Lab splashing out from the boat launch. One of the mothers lowers her sunglasses and surveys the two men—they are unwanted here. Ryan doesn't want to take Carter to his spot, but he is hot and dirty and ready to get in with or without Carter.

Ryan pushes down the path and Carter follows. He doesn't complain, just stumbles along behind Ryan until they pop out at the side of the lake.

A couple of rocks stick out of the water. One is long and flat on top. Ryan's dad used to sit on it and read while Ryan swam around catching minnows in his hands.

It isn't the easiest place to get in the water. It is all slippy rock underfoot, and it gets deep fast. The lake is bigger than most of the freshwater ponds people swim in. There is a lop on the water and the clouds are moving fast across the sky. Ryan strips off, but leaves on the boxers he's wearing and heads in. He walks until the water is waist high then dives under. He swims a few metres underwater then pops up. He can't touch bottom where he is. He looks back and Carter is standing at the edge of the pond. Ryan is filled with irritation that Carter is here. He swims out away from him and then turns around and treads water, looks back to the shore.

Carter is getting in tentatively. He's clumsy on his feet, taking cautious wobbly steps, he is only in up to his knees. Ryan lies back and bobs over a couple of waves. He looks back and Carter is in up to his waist. A big wave comes, and splashes Ryan, he coughs a little. He closes his eyes and clears his throat. He doesn't panic. He is confident in his buoyancy. Ryan opens his eyes just in time to see the wave knock Carter over. His arms flailing, he goes under, then pops up. Ryan expects him to cry out from the cold, but Carter is strangely silent. He must be only a few feet from where he could stand with his head and torso out of the water, the lake gets deep fast, there are sudden dipping holes close to shore. Carter must be in one. The way he is moving is taking him out further, not closer to shore.

Ryan is slow to comprehend what is happening. Surely, Carter can swim. His head disappears below the waterline once more and he comes up facing Ryan, and even at this distance—Ryan must be twenty metres away—he can see the terror in Carter's face. He hesitates for just a moment. An image of himself, sitting alone on the rocks, looking into the empty water where Carter is now, passes through his mind. He shakes his head fast and starts moving. He is doing the front crawl towards Carter, dipping his face in, then breathing to the side, his fingers squeezed together slicing efficiently through the water. He is about five metres away when another wave comes and Carter sinks under it and is pushed into deeper water. This time he doesn't resurface.

Ryan can see Carter fighting underneath the water. Like a human weed, stuck to the bottom of the lake and reaching its tendrils towards the light, unable to crack the surface. He swims behind him and grabs Carter and pulls. Carter is fighting him, but they are just in a dip, a pockmark on the bottom of the lake, it will only take a little for Ryan to drag Carter a few feet away from where he is, to where he will be able to stand. Ryan drags him up and out of the hole. Carter keeps struggling and Ryan keeps hauling Carter along, swimming with him, his hands latched under Carter's armpits, until they are grounded up against the shore. They lie at the water's edge, Carter in Ryan's arms, their legs in the water. Ryan's back lying against the flat rocks on shore. Carter is pushed up against Ryan's chest, between his arms. He is still conscious, but he is coughing up water. When he stops coughing, he strokes Ryan's arm, very softly from his wrist to just above his elbow.

"Thanks, buddy."

"It's nothing," Ryan says. He stops Carter's hand from travelling further up his arm with his own. He pats Carter's hand gently twice, then gets up decisively. Ryan inhales once and wonders if he should say something to Carter, but he looks at Carter's face and it is closed and guarded.

~

Joseph has drilled it into Ryan and Carter: "Always wear your gloves!" Usually, they comply. Bags split and ooze. Viscous substances are smeared on the outside of things—leakages, rotting meat, vomit, blood, all kinds of shit, human and other. You don't have to cover your garbage bags out here, and sometimes the seagulls get at them, or rats, or stray dogs. They don't pick up garbage if the gulls have gone wild, split the bags and spread the garbage out, but if it is only a big tear, they will throw it in the truck. Ryan's gloved thumb slips through a hole in a bag and into something unknown and soft. He pulls his thumb out. It is coated in a brown slick. Ryan rubs his thumb on the grass, but the substance has an oily texture, the smell coming from it gaggingly familiar. Used diapers have their own distinct stench. He takes off both his gloves and throws them into the back of the compactor. He stretches out his hands, and feels relief at their freedom from the sweaty gloves.

The lupins are out, they push up their showy flowered shafts of purple, pink, yellow, and white in ditches and on the most barren of verges on the side of the road. Their leaves spread and catch dewdrops in the morning, and hold up little rounded globes of shimmering water towards the sky like offerings. The lupins fill empty lots with a profusion of colour and a smell that makes Ryan breathe deeply. The three men are on a break and the engine of the garbage truck is turned off. Ray is sitting in the front seat smoking out the window. Carter is leaning against the back of the truck swigging from a bottle of blue Gatorade. Ryan stands in front of the empty lot filled with blossoming flowers, breathing in the peppery alive smell of them, watching bees climb into enveloping petals and emerging with their pollen sacs filled.

He can hear the bees, he can hear birds, he can hear the schoolyard sounds of children in the distance. He used to pick lupins and play swords with them when he was a kid. He would strip them of their coloured petals and throw them in the air like they were confetti.

Lupins are an invasive species. Ryan ponders their ability to thrive in this harsh environment, how they are one of the first flowers to grow after volcanic eruptions, replacing nitrogen in the soil. Their seeds are toxic to humans despite their resemblance to peas.

They finish their morning break and Ray starts the truck back up. Ryan and Carter get back up on the truck and Ray pulls around the corner. Ryan and Carter leap off from their perches with an almost choreographed ease. They are all in sync today. They gather bags with a symmetry. From a bird's-eye view, they would appear to be engaged in a complex dance. Even Ray is in something that resembles a good mood. He is singing along to the radio.

Carter calls out a greeting to old Mrs. Thorne, out for a walk, wearing a blue head scarf against the sun, shuffling along slow with her cane on the other side of the road.

"Grand day!" Carter projects his words into the air with the flourish of a preacher.

Mrs. Thorne nods and her voice comes out louder than Ryan and Carter expect from her bird-like body. "Glorious! A glorious day," she calls out. Ryan is distracted. He is looking up smiling at Carter and Mrs. Thorne who are momentarily delighted with each other. He doesn't look at the bag he is picking up, just reaches down and grabs it. The broken glass is at the top and pierces through the plastic, and cuts cleanly into his hand.

He feels wet, drops the bag, and holds up his hand. He sees the slick of red covering his palm. The lip of the broken glass has cut deep into his hand, between his forefinger and thumb. It has cut right to the bone of his thumb. He doesn't say anything, it is important to him that Mrs. Thorne's glory is not ruined by the blood pouring from him. He is standing with his hand in front of him in clear focus, but everything outside of that is blurred.

"Fuck." Ryan hears Carter breathe in the word, then Carter is grabbing him by the wrist holding his bleeding hand in the air and dragging him along past the houses on the street. He hears Ray behind them calling out, "What's happening?"

Carter ignores Ray. He pulls Ryan towards a house and opens the door without knocking. He pulls Ryan into a kitchen that Ryan remembers vaguely from his childhood. The cabinets' pale wood with spiralled metal handles.

Carter grabs paper towel and tries inadequately to stop the blood. He is calling out, "Evie, Evie, I need your help. Right fucking now, Evie!"

Everything is fuzzy like the old-fashioned TV screen his grandfather had in the shed when Ryan was a kid. His grandfather played hockey games on it, listening more than watching the snowy and sometimes lined screen. Evie is like an animated figure moving across this screen. A sudden flash of colour, a glossy magazine photograph pasted onto a black-and-white collage of newspaper. She is wearing a short green T-shirt with *Living My Best Life* printed across it in fuzzy yellow letters, and black yoga pants. Her hair is tied up on top of her head and she is barefoot.

~

Ryan glances at Carter, he is grey, the colour of a slate beach stone, stained with salt water and dried in the sun.

"Carter, on the couch. Stick your head between your knees," Evie is telling Carter as she advances on Ryan and holds his hand by the wrists examining Carter's handiwork. She tuts and glances around the kitchen. She lets go of Ryan's hand,

"Keep it up," she says as she takes off her shirt, exposing a camouflage sports bra, and tightly ties her T-shirt as a bandage around Ryan's hand.

She leaves Ryan for a moment, and returns wearing an oversized red T-shirt. This one says *Beast Mode* across the front, Ryan catches a whiff of Carter's scent coming from it. She has car keys in her hand and ushers him into the passenger seat of a small car.

When Ryan is released, Evie is still waiting for him at the hospital. His hand is a bandaged club.

Evie drives Ryan home. When she drops him at his parents, he comes around to the driver's window she has wound down. Ryan's hand pulses with pain. He rests his good hand on the window. As he looks in at her, it happens again, Evie is in technicolour and the rest of the world seems in black and white.

"You okay?" Evie asks.

"Glorious!" Ryan says. "I'm glorious, thanks to you," then he goofily waltzes towards the house. He does a strange twirl and tips an imaginary top hat at her before heading to the front door. His mother opens the door with a hand over her mouth looking at the bandages.

Evie is home alone when a knock comes at the door and she peeps through the spy hole. All she can see are flowers, those spiky ones that grow up beside the highway. She opens the door and there is Ryan, a salt-beef bucket full of the things.

Evie feels it, when he looks at her, a kind of heat. It's not the pass-over assessment she has had before from Carter's friends, this is something else, a kind of worship. He tries to put the bucket of flowers on the counter, but they are too big and don't fit under the cabinets. A few petals have already fallen off and Evie can imagine her mom already, "What are all these weeds doing in here? They'll be full of bugs."

"Bring them in here." She gestures to Ryan and he follows her into her bedroom. She sweeps a bra, and a stuffed unicorn from her dresser and Ryan puts the plastic bucket of flowers on top. They are standing facing each other. Evie grabs his bandaged hand and surveys it with a critical eye.

"How does it feel?" she asks.

"It throbs," Ryan says. The word bounces around them.

Evie drops his bandaged hands. She picks up his other hand and kisses his palm, then she sucks slowly on his thumb. Ryan draws it from between her lips and let it rest on her lower lip, pulling it gently down, like he is asking her a question.

This is not like sex has been before for Evie. For one thing, she is completely sober and Ryan can only use one hand. Evie has control of this situation, and she discovers she likes this. It is she that leads Ryan to her bed, it is she that undresses first him, then pulls off her own clothes. Ryan is lying back on the bed. His eyes are closed and she waits until he opens them before she eases herself down onto him. It is her hips that decide the pace. Ryan reaches up and traces her nipple with his good hand, and Evie leans back and lets herself go. Ryan quakes beneath her.

Evie leaves the flowers on her dresser until all of the petals have dropped. She sweeps the beige and limp remains up and ditches the water from the salt-beef bucket. She drives to Ryan's to return the bucket. It is not Ryan, but his mother who opens the door. She eyes Evie and the bucket with suspicion. "Tell Ryan, I came by," Evie says.

"Of course, dear," his mother says, but Evie doesn't think she will.

CHANTERELLE SEASON

~

The ATV trail is along where the old railway tracks used to be, running like an aging scar through the landscape. Susie walks alone along the trail, jumps over a ditch of stagnant water at the side of the path and pushes through alder to get in deep amongst spiky pine trees. She staggers up a short but steep slope to stand on the treed ridge where the mushrooms grow. The basket she is carrying catches on branches. She and Evelyn bought it together at a craft fair. Locally made and outrageously priced. An Instagrammable status symbol amongst Newfoundland's queer and artistic elites. The forest floor here is a carpet of thick luxurious moss. Off-road vehicles rumble along the trail, she hears them coming and feels them shake the earth, inhales drifts of gasoline, but all she can see are quick flashes of their drivers' helmeted heads going by.

She can smell the chanterelles before she sees them, fresh, feral, and redolent of sex. The mushrooms lie nestled in the moss like orange jewels. She plans to fry them in butter, eat them, and cry. It is a relief they are here. She was worried someone else might have snatched them, stripped the place out, taking more than they need. People posted pictures of huge harvests, they would pick every mushroom in sight, even sad slug-eaten specimens, still tiny embryonic fungi, more than anyone could reasonably cook and enjoy.

She takes photographs before she picks the chanterelles. She has a vision of their labial beauty enlarged against a background of green moss. She can feel the strokes she will make with her brush. The almost living nature of the paint itself as it adheres to the canvas. Up close, the moss is a jungle of ferny fronds, and little stalks that reach up and dangle spores are like open reaching hands.

A sad desire is filling her. Desire and memory. The day she and Evelyn found this place, they were happy. The usual concerns—debt, existential dread, how long the roof would last—they had put aside. Their skin was warm. Their bodies had been freed for weeks from winter clothes. Skin and hair softened and gilded from saltwater swimming and sun. It was a physical relief to be allies with the elements and not in conflict with them as they were during the relentless winter and bitter disappointing spring. They had made love in the morning; summer sex with no need for the heavy duvet whose negotiation was a necessity for nine months of the year. The window had been cracked open, a light breeze caressing them. The only damper on their passion was fear of the neighbours hearing them crying out, and a brief interruption when the dog attempted to climb up on the bed with them and investigate the proceedings.

Later, the same day, in the clearing, Evelyn had reached for her again. They were hungry for each other like they had been when they were twenty and missed endless classes and parties because it was painful to be apart. When the feel of Evelyn's knee rubbing against hers in the darkness of some art-house theatre or student dive bar or lecture on *Mrs Dalloway* would make her wet. All information less important than Evelyn's physical presence. Back then they were immersed in the utter selfishness of love, ignoring family, friends, unwashed dishes, and very dirty sheets. Their talk flowed and flowed, sometimes all through the night. Their voices and vaginas both ached pleasurably from excessive use.

Evelyn was a few feet away when she reached out for Susie as they stood amongst the chanterelles, but as Susie walked towards her a tree branch had flicked painfully across her eye. Another, a brittle piney branch, had poked uninvited into her ear, then snapped. Susie had seen a slug. A big one, the kind that exuded blood and yellow guts if you stepped on it. She was aware of the grit, pine needles, bits of leaves and moss collected between her breasts. She felt an annoying itch. Then came ATVs, a convoy of at least eight, the front one playing the radio, reporting loudly on a drunk-driving incident that had claimed two lives over the weekend. The moment was lost.

She thinks of this with such regret. If they had simply waited until the ATVs had passed. If she had guided Evelyn a few steps away from the slug. If she had then sucked softly on the lobe of Evelyn's ear, maybe then Evelyn would be here now.

Susie kneels down, her fingers sink into the moss, they firmly grasp around the stem of a mushroom. She has a need for release that makes her consider rubbing up against the rough bark of the trees around her, or taking off her clothes and grinding herself against the welcoming ground. She can't remember the last time she was touched by another human. She is wet from memory and hormones and sunshine, when she hears the dirt bikes coming down the trail. Their intrusion fills her with a quick flash of rage.

The bikes stop just up the path from her, she lies down. It is an instinct. She lies down with her face hiding in the moss. She keeps still, but her heart is beating fast, just like in childhood games of hide-and-seek, and she can hear it in her ears. She feels her pulse in her left hand where her fist is tightly wrapped around her thumb.

She hears a rustling in the trees. A voice, a boy's, calling out, "I just gotta pee." She hears him struggling through the trees, then the stream of his piss. He is close enough that she hears the sound of his zip as he does up his jeans but the trees are thick and she is hidden.

"What took you so long?" she hears a girl ask. But the girl doesn't wait for an answer, she is impatient revving the engine on her dirt bike.

When they are gone, Susie stands, brushes the moss off herself and pushes out to the trail, clutching her basket full of mushrooms.

Kev sees Susie emerging from the woods. He has noted the car parked up next to the trailhead. It seemed benign, berry pickers, Kev figured. He is waiting for Joseph here at a dead end. His truck pulled off the road. Skeeter is in the passenger seat, lying down audibly snoring. Kev will walk him once he has talked to Joseph. Susie doesn't see Kev; he is parked behind her and she is lost in thought. She places a basket in the back of the car. There is a pretension to that basket that irks Kev. He sees Susie shove her hands in the pockets of her jeans and pull out her car keys, and he also catches the flash of light reflecting off something falling out of her pocket. He is surprised when she doesn't bend to pick it up.

Kev is distracted by Joseph walking towards him, hands trying to look loose, like he is out for a stroll. As if Joseph ever went for a recreational walk. Joseph stops beside Kev's window, he rolls it down and they talk this way, like they are just shooting the shit after an unexpected encounter. Kev smiles and stares out his window and they finalize a deal. Nothing big, just a few issues Kev is having with a supplier that he hopes a word from Joseph can work out. Joseph reaches in and pets Skeeter, bangs on the roof of the truck before he walks away.

Kev waits until Joseph is out of sight. He scrolls through his phone, sends his mom a picture of Skeeter, tongue lolling out and wearing a goofy dog smile.

Susie is gone, but he can see the glint of something shiny on the verge where she dropped it. He gets out of his car and whistles to Skeeter who jumps out of the truck and walks beside him. Kev half expects to find the foil wrapper from a chocolate bar, but lying there is a key. A house key on a plain ring, no identifiable marks. He picks it up and looks around. He knows that Susie lives alone; heard his mom gossiping about the other one not coming back, about seeing Susie at the Needs buying four bottles of wine on a Tuesday. He doubts Susie has given the spare key to anyone. He doesn't want to freak her out by showing up with the key. He rubs the key between his thumb and fingers. He considers dropping it where he found it, leaving it sticking up in some way that draws attention to it in case she comes back. She is an adult, she would figure out how to get into her home, and who knows maybe it isn't locked. Maybe she dropped that key on purpose. We all need to ditch evidence of our past sometimes. Maybe the key was the other woman's, her girlfriend, or wife, or whatever, and Susie was losing it so she didn't have to look at it. His mom said she'd been seen late at night walking around shoving stuff in garbage cans.

Maybe the key was part of some greater ritualistic purge, but the thought bugs him, her trying to get into her house, that old dog of hers barking from the inside, not understanding why dinner is late. Kev whistles for Skeeter who comes bounding out of the woods where he's been sniffing around and heads back to the truck.

When he parks up in front of her house, Susie has all four doors of the cars open and is peering under seats. He steps out from the truck, instructs Skeeter to stay, and walks towards her, the key dangling from his finger.

"I think you lost this," Kev says and holds it out. She hesitates for a moment before reaching out for it. Kev is working on relaxing his shoulders, using what his mom refers to as his puppy-dog eyes. He holds the key out but doesn't step forward. Like with Skeeter, he has to remain still and let her take the treat and prove he would never lash out.

"Thanks," Susie replies, her eyes lingering on the tattoos on his face. Before she can ask the obvious questions, "Where did you find it? How do you know it is mine?"

a delivery van pulls up, the driver filling the air with noise as he opens the metal back of the van and puts down a ramp.

The driver nods to Susie.

"Just leave it on the porch," she says.

"You want a hand?" Kev asks the guy who is tipping a large box up onto a dolly. The guy gives Kev the once-over then shakes his head. Doesn't say a word to him. Susie looks anxious for them both to leave. But Kev is pissed at the way the delivery driver looked at him. He is the good guy in this situation, there was no need to dismiss him so rudely. Buddy didn't even have the decency to say, "No, thanks." Kev looks at the basket resting beside the car.

"Blueberries?" he asks.

"Chanterelles."

"Mushrooms? You sure they're safe?" Kev wouldn't have eaten one of those weird-looking things if he was starving to death. They look like cut-off ears.

"I'm sure."

The box is on the porch now. Blocking it off.

"Thanks," Susie calls to the driver who nods again and glares at Kev. He doesn't know the guy, but clearly he knows who Kev is and doesn't approve. His face showed up in the paper after his last arrest. He doesn't believe in covering himself up when he gets hauled into court. The journalists want a picture, they'll find one. Better not to look like a baby playing peekaboo with a blanket in front of the TV cameras.

"You need help with that, getting it inside?"

"No, I'll be fine." But the box looks large, unwieldy, and impossible to get through the door. "I'll organize things, then bring it in."

The rains starts then, sparse but heavy drops of water.

"Let me help," Kev says. "It will only take a minute."

When she opens the door, her dog Sam comes out and beelines for Kev. When Susie tries to call him in, Sam ignores her, throws himself on his back and Kev squats and rubs his belly. Skeeter whines jealously from the truck. Susie climbs over the couch in its box and puts the chanterelles inside the door.

She manages to lure the dog in, and away from Kev, with a treat, and shuts him in the kitchen with the cats. The rain is starting to come down hard. Even under the protection of the porch roof Kev, Susie and the cardboard box are getting wet. They get stuck halfway through, the wet cardboard catching on the door frame. "Get out of the way," Kev says, and gives the thing one huge push which sends it through the door and he stumbles after it. The rain is coming down fast, driven through the door by the wind.

Susie shuts the door against it, shutting Kev inside with her. They are hot, and wet with rainwater, and Susie can smell Kev: male sweat, cigarettes, and cheap laundry detergent, mingling with the scent of the basket of mushrooms. The rain is torrential. Kev has no intention of doing it, but there is something about the raggedness of her breathing that makes him hard. And when he reaches out and pulls her body in, she doesn't resist, she responds.

This is fucking; the fast food of sex. Susie always considered sex with men to be like this, fulfilling a desire quickly with minimal effort or time, and you often felt gross a few hours afterwards.

They are standing up, her back painfully jammed up against a door frame. Her pants off completely, his around his ankles. He is young, strong, and wildly inappropriate and all these things turn her on. There is no sentimentality here, only the mutual desire to get off fast.

As she comes, she moans partly with relief, and partly with worry about catching syphilis.

It is awkward afterwards. She gets her jeans back on quickly. They share a half hug at the door then Kev leaves, the rain has eased a little. Susie sits on the wet couch box, for a moment she thinks she might cry, but she doesn't. She laughs and laughs and laughs. When she lets the dog and cats out of the kitchen, they sniff around her with judgmental faces.

She puts the couch together. It is deep green and velvet. She sets it up in her studio. She showers, washing off Kev, the smell of wet cardboard, moss, and the pine needles that fell into her cleavage while she was in the woods. After her shower, she cooks the chanterelles in butter, pours herself a glass of white wine. She sits on her couch and eats. When she is done eating, she calls Evelyn.

LITTLE BITCH

~

We look alike, Mom says. She says, when I turn nineteen, we'll go to the bars in St. John's together and tell everyone we're sisters.

I haven't lived with Mom since I was just a baby. I live with my dad's parents. Mom used to come around to their place for visits when I was little, but when I was around five, she stole some cash from Nan's purse, and she got barred.

Sometimes she would stand across the road and watch me, Cody, and Braydon playing. Cody lives next door and when the weather was good, we were always out on his driveway going round and round on our tricycles. Cody used to go, "Zoom zoom," Braydon used to keep ringing his bell, but not me. I focused on pedalling and I was always fastest. Mom would stand there watching us and we would wave at her, or stick out our tongues, sometimes give her the finger. If Nan saw her, she would yell across the street and threaten Mom with a restraining order.

Then she just stopped showing up and I didn't see her for months until the day Nan and I ended up in the waiting room at the doctor's office and she was there too. I walked in and she called out, "Oh Tyra, you look so beautiful. Come give Mommy a hug." Nan made me sit in the furthest seat from her and said loudly, "Don't you make trouble, Lisa-Marie." Everyone else in the waiting room was silent, staring at their feet, or the poster about the signs of juvenile diabetes. "Does your child need to go to the bathroom a lot?" Mom stopped talking, but when I snuck a glance at her she was staring at me and crying. She was pregnant, her belly huge.

Nan says she doesn't hate my mom, she just doesn't trust her. She used to go visit Mom every year at Christmas. She'd take a homemade cherry cake and my latest school portrait already done up in a frame.

I knew Mom lived in the apartments just two blocks from our house. I had seen her sitting outside on a picnic table smoking, ashing her cigarette into a rusty coffee can filled with cigarette butts. There was always a collection of plastic toys out front, a playhouse, some slides, and a sandbox that all the kids who lived in the place and the local cats used.

I had just turned twelve when I showed up at her place one afternoon. She was really happy to see me. She cried and everything. She had photographs of me and her other kids up on her walls. She had a calico kitten for a while, until it went into heat and ran away. I went there every day after school, until Justin moved in.

After he arrived all the pictures of me on her living-room wall were slightly askew and there was always a car battery sitting on a bunch of old newspapers in the middle of the coffee table. She was twitchy. One time, she wouldn't let me in and I heard Justin say, "That girl's got no manners, doesn't she know to call before she comes over?" She had a broken window and a bunch of bruises on her neck the next time I saw her.

Sometimes when I was over, Justin would be too nice to me. Give me twenty bucks, and tell me how much I looked like Mom.

"Why are you with a little bitch like him?" Justin asked me once when I came by with Cody. And Cody, he is such a little bitch, he didn't even try to defend himself. Justin looked over my body long and slow, lingering over my chest and nodding in approval. Cody just stood there grinning like having Justin drool over me was some kind of compliment.

Justin got a job out West and took off. Left Mom with rent to pay and a damaged apartment. She got evicted and that's when she moved to Paradise. I haven't seen her in a long time. She texts me. Sometimes, when her phone's working.

No one was seeing anyone when Covid started. The school closed, the streets were empty, and there were never any cops. It's like they were too afraid of catching the virus to actually try and arrest anyone. Me, Cody, and Braydon started going out every day on our dirt bikes. We pulled wheelies and jumped the speed bumps and raced right down the main streets of the town. It was awesome. While everyone else was all stressed out, we were having a blast.

Nan told me I shouldn't be hanging out with Cody and Braydon, that I was supposed to be staying home. She said I was going to get Covid and then she and Pop would get it and die. "Take more than some virus to kill you, Nan," I said to her.

She tried to give me a curfew but I just climbed out the window. "You're not my mother," I said to her, and there wasn't much that she could say to that. Pop, he didn't know what to do with me, he just shook his head and headed out to the shed if I started kicking off. It was too much, us all being in the house together all the time.

Kev hired us a few months after it all started. We were supposed to be doing online classes, but only Braydon kept up with them. Cody had two younger brothers and there was only one laptop between them, so his mom gave up nagging him. The three of us were racing down Water Street. I was in the lead and I had just come down from doing a cat walk and I ran a stop sign. Cody was behind me, and he ran the stop sign too, but Kev Babcock was turning onto Water Street when Cody hit the intersection and he almost took Cody out. Cody veered into the side of the road and his bike tilted so bad I thought he was going to come off it. He managed to right himself and stopped at the side of the street. Kev had pulled out to avoid him and pulled back over and parked his truck right up in front of Cody, blocking him. He jumped out of his truck looking mad as hell. Braydon stopped behind Cody. I circled back, but kept a little distance.

"You'll get yourselves killed, riding like that. I could report you, you know? Dangerous driving. And how old are you all? You fucking idiots!" Kev was ranting. Cody and Braydon looked like they were going to shit themselves, they were saying nothing, waiting for me to take charge like always.

I took off my helmet. "It's us should be calling the cops, Cocky, b'y. You weren't looking where you were going."

Kev looked me up and down. "Oh yeah," he said. "So, if we look at your boy's GoPro, who do you think the cops are gonna side with?" But he was scratching his head and looking less mad. I don't think he was used to people talking back to him. "I'll make you a deal," Kev said. And that was how we started working for him.

The first few deliveries we did for Kev were just small ones. He got us to drop off cigarettes at his mom's. A bottle of rum to some old uncle of his. He told us later that was a test, to see if we would deliver the rum, or if we'd just drink it. He didn't pay us and I was pissed off.

That night just after midnight, I snuck out of my bedroom window and walked over to Kev's place. The security lights came on and I crouched low on the far side of Kev's truck. He didn't open his door. That thing must have turned on every time a cat walked by. When the lights went off again, I dug my keys into the side of his truck and made one long scratch. The noise made my teeth hurt. I didn't tell anyone about it.

It was still there when Kev flagged us down a few weeks later and that's when we started doing real work. At first, we didn't look inside the packages Kev gave us, just handed them over to the customer and took the money. It was me that finally eased one open and figured out how much we could take. A pill here. A little pinch of powder there. Not too much, and not all the time. I figured out pretty fast who we could give a light package to, the more fucking desperate someone is, the easier it is to fuck them over. If someone is fucked up, they won't know if they took that pill and can't remember, or if you shorted them. Once we had some stock of our own, I started building my own customer base. Kids our age, not yet buying from Kev. Sometimes, if we didn't have anything in our stash, I'd sell them one of Pop's expired painkillers from when he hurt his back. No one ever complained.

Cody was all nervous at first. “I don’t want to get in trouble, Tyra.” He just wanted to play it straight with Kev. But then after we got away with it for a couple of weeks, he wanted to skim a bit more, but I told him no. Him and Braydon started talking big, but I was the one that made the decisions. I pointed out they didn’t want to get on Kev’s bad side. We’d all heard stories, knew that once the cops found a baseball bat with nails hammered into it in the back of his truck. The evidence got lost and the charges were dropped. That was the kind of guy Kev was, the kind who could make things disappear from an evidence locker, and we had to be careful.

Kev wasn’t paying us enough. He was treating our deliveries like we were on a paper round. He assumed Cody was somehow in charge of me and Braydon and always talked to him. Cody didn’t really get the risk we were taking for Kev. For him it was just playing at dealing. He spent the money he made on video games, and candy bars. He wanted to order one of those hoverboards like a fucking six-year-old. As if his parents wouldn’t want to know how he could afford it. I kept telling him he had to take this shit seriously. Working for Kev, that was a chance for him to make it, not end up working as a janitor or a frigging flag man stuck out on the highway in all fucking weather holding a sign, like his dad.

We didn’t get much trouble from customers. April Mathews tried to get away without paying. We were in her house, me, Cody and Braydon, wearing the black face masks Kev gave us. I made the boys wear them, because we looked tougher in them, and I really didn't want to make Nan and Pop sick. I grabbed a pair of scissors from April's kitchen counter and threatened to drive them through her hand if she didn't find the money. She found it real fast then. After that I reminded the b'ys every time, money first, doesn't matter how bad someone is sweating and shaking, or if they're your friend or your uncle. No drugs until you get the cash.

Kev dismissed me before he asked Cody about the other job. "I gotta talk business with your man. You better get on home, Tyra, this might take a while."

"Sure, Kev," I said.

"Good girl," he said. Fuck him. I waited around the corner.

Cody didn't want to do it. He told Kev he'd think about it.

I said to him after, "What the fuck, Cody? You can't turn down that kind of shit. He's going to think you're such a pussy."

The next day, when we met Kev to pick up some product, I heard Kev say, "You decide on that other job?"

"I'll do it," Cody said. I had told him to negotiate. We could have made at least a thousand with the risk the job involved, but Cody got so nervous he just took the wad of cash Kev paid him up front without saying anything else.

We didn't tell Braydon. "Better he doesn't know," I told Cody. I made him swear to keep it between us.

Braydon was already getting nervous about the dealing. A couple of times we showed up to his house and he'd already taken off somewhere without us, gone fishing, or he was out with his dad getting wood. His mom never liked me much.

"We're doing that fucker a favour. Cleaning up the mess in his yard," I heard Kev tell Cody. "No one's going to get hurt." But I saw a little twitch in his eyebrow. I'd seen that before when he told Cody we'd get no trouble from April.

He wanted Cody to set a fire. To burn up the crap in Justin's yard. I knew Kev's dog used to be Justin's, and I didn't need to know any more. Justin was a waste of space. I was happy to get him back for whatever he done to Kev. He probably owed him money.

The night we went to do the job, I told Nan I was going to Cody's to watch a movie. Nan just nodded, her and Pop were watching *Wheel of Fortune*. They always get the answers before the contestants.

Cody was all shaky. "I don't know, Tyra, it doesn't feel right. And how does Kev know that house is empty? I mean, how does he know for sure?"

"You can't just say you'll do something for Kev, then not do it. He'll beat the shit outta you for sure, maybe worse. Anyway, it's not your job to worry, your job is just to do what Kev asks. Remember, you're a soldier. You don't question commands." I knew turning it into a game, like when we were kids, and used to pretend we were on a mission looking for terrorists, that Cody would go for it.

Justin's was a few blocks from where we lived, but it felt like it took us forever to get there. It was rainy and no one else was out. We left the TV on in the basement and snuck real quietly out the back door, no one would know we had gone. At ten-thirty, Cody's mom would always call down and tell me it was time for me to go home. "Night, Mrs. Payne," I'd call out as I was leaving, then I'd see her curtain twitch making sure I was actually crossing over the lawn to my house. I knew we had to be back by nine-thirty, just in case she called down early.

Cody had filled up a gas can earlier in the week. It was normal for us to do that and no one at the Ultramar was surprised to see him. I made Cody carry the can underneath his oversized sweatshirt just in case. The weather was bad, wet leaves were falling down from the trees and one of those winds that whipped everything around screeched constantly. It was too hot for this time of year and I was sweating, my hair was getting all misty.

We came down the back alley, then skirted into Justin's yard from the neighbour's. Justin's yard was a mess. Cody went to put on the flashlight on his phone, but I realized what he was doing and stopped him. He started to whine and I said, "Shut up, Cody. No talking."

"Jesus, Tyra, Justin's truck is here. He could be inside," Cody hissed at me and I put my finger to my lips.

His truck was there, backed right next to the house.

I stopped for a minute. I couldn't hear anything. No signs of life. Then a car came down the street and I said to Cody, "Get down now," and we both lay down on the ground until the car was gone. Cody pulled the gas can out from his sweater and put it on the grass beside him.

"I don't like this, Tyra," he said.

"Go home, then," I told him.

"Tyra, don't be like that."

"Go, I mean it. Get!" I said to him. I saw him start to cry and then he left. He just fucking left me there.

Kev would be pissed if the job wasn't done. I wasn't even sure if Kev thought Cody was up for it. The whole thing was probably some kind of test. If Cody didn't follow through, his ass would be Kev's, and of course, the money Kev had paid us was already gone.

I thought I heard something from inside the house. That hack-hack of the smoker's cough I knew Justin had, but it could have come from any of the houses. It could have been my imagination.

I crept closer to the house and poured gas around Justin's truck and some shells of ATVs he had close to it. Kev was right, the place needed cleaning up. I pooled some by Justin's side door.

I turned around, lit a match, and threw it over my shoulder. I decided I'd leave it up to fate to see if the thing caught. I didn't see it, but I heard it. Just a crackle almost like pattering rain at first. I caught a whiff of burning gas and leaves, and then there was a small explosion followed by a rushing sound like waves coming up on the shore. As I was running away there was a chemical smell of plastic in the air and I felt the warmth on my back as the flames rose. I glanced back only once, I could see the glow around Justin's yard. Then a flame licking up into the sky.

I headed over to Cody's. He was watching *Top Gun*. He didn't say anything to me. I slipped down on the couch beside him and rested my head on his shoulder. After a few minutes he put his arm around me. We heard sirens, and the sound of explosions that lasted for a while. It sounded like fireworks.

HELP

~

On the highway, just outside of St. John's, Evelyn looked over her shoulder, checking before she switched lanes, and that was when he came stumbling out of the ditch dividing the east- and westbound traffic.

At first, Susie thought he was an animal. Then, briefly, as her mind tried to make sense of things, she pondered, *hitchhiker*. He was on one leg and two hands, and then he was standing up. He spun around once, a complete circle as if trying to find his bearings, then he turned to face the oncoming traffic. He was waving his arms flagging them down and walking haphazardly into the centre of the road, and Susie was shouting at Evelyn.

"Fuck, stop, he's hurt. We're gonna hit him."

Evelyn slammed on the brakes, just stopping the car before she mowed the guy down. Both of their brains were trying to make sense of the man limping towards their car. He was gesturing at them still, looking terrified and terrifying, and yelling, "Help."

There was nowhere he could conceivably have come from, no evidence of a car crashed or broken down. He wasn't carrying a bag or backpack. He was wearing a ripped white T-shirt, grey jogging pants, and had a pair of mirrored sports sunglasses perched on his head. It was a Saturday, in the middle of the day, the conditions were fine, and cars were heading in either direction, but no one else stopped.

"Help. Help me." It was so rare to hear those words in earnest, and not flung around by school kids playing at disaster. The man yelled these words at them and they were urgent.

Ideas flitted through Susie's mind: hit by a car, ATV accident, psychotic break. Evelyn put on the four-way flashers and Susie's hand was already opening up her door.

As she was getting out of the passenger seat two things happened: firstly, she remembered the story of the man on bath salts eating another man's face, and, secondly, the guy stuck his hand in his pocket and pulled something red out, and brandished it at her. What she thought she saw was a hypodermic needle, and she was getting back in the car fast, and Evelyn was locking the doors.

"Holy shit, he's got a syringe!" Susie yelled, the guy kept coming.

"Help, I broke my foot. I need help." His face was contorted, his mouth twisting as it formed words, and his eyebrows were arched up, like the exaggerated features of a horror mask.

"Show me what's in your pocket!" Evelyn yelled.

"It's a lighter. It's just a lighter," he shouted. He was right beside Susie's window, he had bent down and was peering in at them, his face level with hers. He waved the lighter in front of the window. His eyes were darting from side to side, he managed to focus in on them only for a moment before his eyes started moving frenetically once more.

"Show me again!" Evelyn shouted, but he'd shoved the red thing back in his pocket, and he was so unsteady that this movement hadn't been easy for him.

"It's just a lighter," Susie found herself saying, although she wasn't sure.

Evelyn pressed unlock and as soon as they all heard the click, the guy was climbing in the back seat before Susie could get out and help him.

"Okay, it's going to be okay, buddy," Susie said.

She and Evelyn had picked up strays before. They had experience taming feral cats and one of their dogs had had trust issues when they adopted her from Animal Services. The day they took her home, she had bitten Evelyn and drawn blood. There was a time they had rescued a large snapping turtle from the middle of a highway in Northern Ontario. The turtle was the size of a toilet seat. Susie remembered the sound it made after Evelyn had grabbed the back of its shell to lift it off the road, the audible snap as its jaws came together so close to Evelyn's hand. That day, at least, the turtle didn't get hit by a car.

"We'll take you to the hospital," Susie said.

"No, no, take me to Mom's." He was slinking down, keeping his head below the rear windshield.

"Are you sure we shouldn't take you to the hospital?"

"No, just take me to my mom's, she'll take me to hospital."

"What happened to you?" Evelyn asked.

"I broke my foot," was all he answered, and now Susie took him in. He was slouched low in the back of the car, his hand still gripping the door handle, keeping it slightly ajar as if he might need a fast getaway. He had a black eye, a large mauve bruise spread across his chest on the right side of his body, his arm was bleeding, as was his head, and in between his eyebrows. It was clear someone had beaten the shit out of him.

"We've all had a shock. Let's all take a deep breath," Susie said. Then she raised her hands, slowly breathing in, and lowered them, exhaling. The man and Evelyn both breathed with her.

"We'll take you to your mom's," Susie said.

Evelyn was trying to pull the car back out into the road.

"We've gotta get out of here. Just go," the man said.

"I'm just waiting for a break in the traffic." Evelyn spoke in a bright, calm, artificial voice that Susie had last heard when they were hiking and there was a bear up on the trail in front of them. "Oh, look a bear, isn't that nice," Evelyn had said as they both started slowly backing away from it down the trail. It had run away from them into the woods, but the whole way back to the parking lot every twig snap and leaf rustle had sounded like a bear stalking them.

Evelyn pulled out. As she drove, she checked in the rear-view mirror to see if they were being followed.

The guy was draped over Evelyn's suitcase on the seat beside him. He was below the level of the rear windshield and the side windows, keeping his head down. His adrenaline was dropping and pain was kicking in. The skin on his face that wasn't bruised was turning pale yellow.

Susie looked up and saw a highway sign. *Paradise*, it said.

"Does your mom live in Paradise?" she asked.

And he nodded. "Out by the Orange Store."

Evelyn kept calmly driving, and Susie had no idea if she knew where they were going.

"Sorry, but do you have a tissue?" he asked and Susie handed him a wad of napkins from the glove compartment. He dabbed at a small cut on his arm, unaware of the blood dripping down the side of his face and soaking into the back seat of the car.

She introduced herself, as though they were making friends in the schoolyard or at an AA meeting.

"My name is Susie."

"Trevor."

He closed his eyes.

"Are you still with me, Trevor?"

"Yes, my love, I'm just in pain."

"I know, I just need to keep checking you're still conscious."

"Oh, there's the Orange Store," Susie said, like they had just sighted an attraction on the side of the road, Joey Smallwood's Head in Gambo, or the big moose at the rest stop in Whitbourne.

"Just so you know, your door's open a bit," Evelyn said.

Trevor pulled the door shut then, he seemed to have decided he could trust them to take him where he asked.

"We're from Bay Mal Verde. Where are you from?"

"Trepassey."

"I know a guy from Trepassey, Lloyd Butt?" Susie said. Trevor ignored this.

Pain made him blink up at her through rheumy eyes. His sunglasses were still on top of his head, Ray-Bans.

It seemed to be taking forever to get anywhere, it felt like they would be eternally trapped in the car together, with Trevor possibly dying, and all of them trying to trust each other. Trevor trusting them not to take him to the hospital or the police station, and them trusting him not to kill them or attempt to hijack the car. They were all in this together with their collective goal being to get him to his mom's house alive.

"Thanks for helping me," he said again.

"No worries," Susie said, as if she was used to picking up bleeding strangers on the highway. She was realizing now, he must have jumped, or been thrown out of a moving vehicle headed in the other direction.

Evelyn drove on. Trevor squeezed his eyes shut in pain and then opened them and stared up at Susie, blinking at her, like he was trying to remember who she was and why he was here.

Trevor mumbled out some more instructions, told Evelyn to turn left at the next intersection.

If he passed out, what would they do? What if he died in the back of their car? Susie's cell phone was at home attached to the charger. Evelyn's was in her purse on the other side of her suitcase. Susie could not get to it without reaching right across Trevor, and she was afraid if she touched him, he might lash out at her. She was both scared of and scared for him.

"What's the street name?" Evelyn asked.

"Pleasant, it's on Pleasant Street."

"And what's your mom's name? Just in case you faint and we need to find her?"

"Gloria," he said and again squeezed his eyes shut. The closer they were getting the slower time seemed to move. Susie began reading the street names out loud as they passed by them.

"We'll get you home soon. Everything will be fine," she

said. As though maternal love could fix his foot and resolve his issues.

"Thanks again. It's good of you."

"No worries," she responded with bright retail-work insincerity.

How long had they been in the car? She tried to work it out, it felt like hours. Panic was rising in her throat, but she swallowed it down.

"Soon, we'll get you there soon," Susie reassured them all once more. She was trying to quash the thoughts in her head. *What if his foot wasn't broken? What if they were driving him to seek out revenge, to carry out a vendetta? Were they accomplices?* Then she remembered the angle of his foot as he dragged it across the road, it wasn't something you could fake.

"Turn here," Trevor said.

"What number?" Evelyn asked.

"Thirteen."

Susie thought she would start laughing but shook her head, she had to hold back the rising hysteria. Once it started, there was no stopping it.

As they drove down Pleasant Street, a man was out washing his car. At another house a woman was pulling groceries out of the back of her trunk. There were people here, but a sense of despair. No one had flowers growing in their front yard, paint was flaking and bits of siding were missing from some of the houses. At number thirteen, a woman was holding open the driver's door of a black Honda Civic with a cracked and broken patch on the bumper. She was short, dressed in jean shorts and a floral halter top. Her grey-and-blond hair was piled on her head.

"Pull up, pull up. Don't let her leave," Susie said, as Evelyn infuriatingly pulled past the house so she could turn around and be parked in the correct and legal direction.

The woman didn't turn to look at them as Evelyn parked blocking the end of the drive.

She wasn't getting in the car yet. She was organizing her things, with the door open.

"Gloria," Susie yelled, "I have your son Trevor, he has a broken foot."

She didn't turn.

"Gloria!"

Evelyn was helping Trevor out of the car, she had her arm around him and he was limping along.

"Mom!" he called out.

Gloria turned then. Her face was pale, but made up, she had blue eyeliner on her bottom eyelid. The foundation she wore didn't hide the smoker's lines around her mouth. Her eyes flickered briefly over Susie, then she ignored her and looked at her son.

"What's she gone done to you now?"

"We didn't do anything to him. We just found him," Susie said.

Gloria continued to ignore her.

"I broke my foot. Help me, Mom, I broke my foot."

Gloria went to his side and together she and Evelyn began to half carry him towards the steps leading to a door at the side of the house.

It was then that Trevor noticed there was a man in the passenger seat of the Civic.

"Shane, Shane brother, come help me. I broke my foot,"

The man in the car stayed looking forward.

"Shane, Shane b'y, is that you?"

Evelyn and Gloria tried to move him along, but Trevor had stopped co-operating. He was not hopping along with them, but was bending down to look in the car.

"It's not Shane," Gloria said.

"Who is it then?"

"No one," Gloria said.

"Kev? Kev is that you?"

Then a wave of realization and adrenaline swept through Trevor and he hopped out of Evelyn and Gloria's hands towards the car.

"It's you that done this to me, man. You fucking cunt. I'm gonna kill you!"

He hurled his sunglasses at the back of the car and they bounced off making a cracking sound.

"Well, I think we'll leave you to it," Susie said. Evelyn remained standing, a look on her face like she was about to try some mediation tactic.

"Evelyn. We have to go. Now." Evelyn moved then and got back in the car. As they pulled out, Susie glanced back. Trevor was lying on the grass on his side in the fetal position, his hands clasped around his knees, his mouth gaped open in agony. Gloria had deserted him and was headed into the house. Kev had gotten out of the car and was staring after them.

GOOD FRIDAY

~

It was a Friday, which was supposed to be a fun day, but it was Good Friday, which meant everything was closed. It was one of those dissatisfying holidays when you got the day off school but there was nothing to do except feel sad about the death of Jesus.

Tyra sat cross-legged on her bed eating Sweet Sixteen mix. The candies were jewel coloured, unapologetically artificial. Tyra liked the little flat strips of red licorice best, they were always a little hard, but she liked tearing them in half with her teeth. She left all the grape gummies until last, they were her least favourite.

She was thinking about the light-blue pill in her backpack. The pill was in an Advil bottle in the pouch she kept tampons and her birth control in. She didn't know exactly what the pill was, Percocet maybe? She had stolen it a week ago from the school librarian. Ms. Noel had left her purse at her desk when she went to the washroom. Tyra hadn't had time to take a good look at the prescription label on the container, just enough time to notice the name on it wasn't the librarian's. This didn't surprise her; there was something about Ms. Noel that reminded Tyra of her mom. She was unpredictable. She would be joking around with them one minute, asking them if they were watching *Love Is Blind*, then five minutes later, yelling at them to keep the noise down—really angry, not just raising her voice to get their attention, but yelling in the out-of-control way teachers weren't supposed to. Tyra only took the one pill from the fourteen the librarian had left. She didn't even open her wallet to check for cash. The act was one of bravado, the other kids in the library watching her all nervous, a few even disapproving. None of them brave enough to try and get in her way. The pill was more of a trophy than an asset.

Tyra was bored. She had texted Braydon three times, she was sure he had weed. He hadn't texted her back. Cody was away for the weekend with his parents. He always went with them, never even put up a fight when they insisted he go with them. He invited her to come with him once. Like spending the weekend in some place surrounded by his cousins was her idea of a good time.

Cody made her promise not to take the pill unless he was around. He was all nervous about her overdosing.

"I got it from the fucking librarian," she told him.

"But you don't know where the fuck she got it. There's bad shit out there, Tyra. My uncle's friend, Nikki, she died of an overdose two weeks ago and she worked at a preschool. You don't even know what that shit is."

Tyra looked at her phone. Even if Braydon didn't have weed, maybe he could steal some booze from his grandfather. If Braydon didn't text back, she would go out alone and see how fast she could take the back path. She would take off her helmet so she could feel the speed pull at her hair. She shoved a white-and-pink gummy worm into her mouth. She jammed her hand into her jeans pocket and pulled out a lighter. She lit the lighter with her left hand and swept her right pointer finger through the flame.

Tyra texted Braydon once more.

WTF where r u!!!!!!!!!!!!!!!

She heard an ATV coming down Water Street, it was loud with the occasional hiccup in its engine. Tyra turned her head to the noise, she listened. Heard the grind, the acceleration jerky, but not in a showy way, a quirk she knew of Braydon's driving. It was Braydon's dad's ATV, but it was Braydon driving. He used it sometimes instead of his bike. Tyra could identify most of the rides and riders in town. Her ear acutely tuned to the variances of engines and mufflers, she knew by how someone took a turn, cautious or fast, tight to the curb or swooping out close or into the opposite lane, who was driving. Like a bird enthusiast trying to identify a variety of sparrow from its call, Tyra could shut her eyes and listen and know with certainty who was going by. It wasn't something she had learned, it was something she could just do. She looked out her bedroom window, and caught sight of Braydon disappearing away from her house.

Maybe his phone was dead. Maybe he hadn't heard her texts come in. She didn't like it. There had been something about Braydon recently. Something slippery about him. He was her boy. He shouldn't be hiding stuff from her. And if he was, Tyra was going to find out what it was.

Her nan turned on the radio. A Good Friday service was playing. A man was talking about forgiveness. The need to forgive others and to forgive ourselves for misdeeds. Misdeeds sounded like something good you had missed out on. Like the day Tyra skipped school and someone set the dumpster on fire. The police and fire trucks showed up, but they never arrested anyone.

Tyra ate the last candy, then she walked over to her bag, dug around for the pouch inside and pulled out the container of pills. She shook some into her hand then put all the red painkillers back in the bottle. She left the blue pill sitting on her upturned palm. It was the colour of a robin's egg, the blue of the inside of the white mug her social worker always had sitting half full of tea on her desk. The pill looked so innocent, sitting there in her hand. The door to her bedroom started opening up behind her.

"Tyra, you got any laundry?" her nan asked.

Tyra slapped her hand to her mouth and swallowed the pill down fast and dry. She felt it catch in her throat, but forced it down with the sweet saliva in her mouth.

"No, Nan. I'm heading out for a ride."

"Alright, but be back for supper."

Tyra kissed her nan's cheek as she brushed past her. Her nan remained hovering in Tyra's bedroom doorway. Nan looked old today, still in her robe at 10 a.m., her hair flat on one side.

~

The first time Braydon and Carter hooked up was Christmas. Braydon was at a Tibb's Eve party. He hadn't wanted to go, but Tyra and Cody showed up at his house on their way there and dragged him along with them. He felt like the three of them were part of a wheelbarrow. Tyra and Cody couldn't function without him supporting them, a permanent third wheel to balance out their instability. Tyra had brought vodka that night, and that never ended well.

Tyra and Cody had started fighting on the way over. Tyra yelled, Cody cried, then punched a hard concrete retaining wall. Once they arrived, they set about making up in the main downstairs bathroom with a locked door and a lot of moaning. Hannah White had plunked herself down on a couch next to Braydon. She put her hand on his knee. There was a red clot of Dorito powder in the corner of her mouth. Tyra kept telling Braydon that Hannah had a crush on him. Tyra didn't like Hannah. She half joked she wanted Braydon to go out with Hannah so he could get some nudie shots that they could post online.

"No," Braydon had said. "How come you hate her so much anyway?"

Tyra just shrugged. "I don't need a reason." Hannah White came up a lot in Tyra's fights with Cody.

"I'm going for a smoke," Braydon told Hannah, but when he got to the door, he grabbed his jacket from where it was piled up with others on a chair. Outside it was crisp and clear and Braydon had a perfect three-beer buzz on. He didn't even stop for a smoke, just started walking up and away from the noise. He was headed to the cemetery.

Most of the guys that went up there were old. Braydon wasn't interested in guys his dad's age, although he felt a certain comfort, seeing them there, knowing he wasn't the only one.

Younger guys did show up occasionally, from the boats or in town for hockey tournaments. Tonight, he hoped for someone home from university. Bored of watching *The Grinch* with their parents, or getting stoned with their high-school friends, they would head up to the cemetery looking for company, a moment of intimacy up in the trees, a break from whoever they pretended to be in front of their family. Some of those boys were out, but not Braydon. Not here. Not now.

At first when he started coming, the middle-aged men wouldn't get out of their parked cars and Braydon would pretend he hadn't seen them pull into the parking lot, see him, then pull out fast. He would stand staring down at Stevie Loder's grave. Braydon hadn't known him, but remembered when he went missing.

The older guys eventually got used to seeing Braydon. He didn't go to the cemetery often, but often enough they knew he was there for the same purpose as them, not just an accidental interloper on their cruising spot. A few of them had tried to wave Braydon over, but he didn't go with them. If he saw one of those men out in town, filling up his tank with gas, or at church with their wives and kids when his mom dragged him along on holidays, they didn't acknowledge him.

It was a cool night and there was no wind. The thin dusting of snow on the ground was moonlit. The cemetery was high up and when Braydon was at the crest of the hill it was built on, he looked back over the water. He could see Christmas lights twinkling below him and on the other side of the harbour. Some of the boats had lights running up and down their rigging. He didn't recognize the guy, not at first, just felt the hairs on the back of his neck rise with a sense of possibilities. The guy was wearing a baseball cap pulled low, and he was nervous, kept looking over his shoulder.

Nervous could be dangerous, but Braydon wanted to feel hot breath on his throat. He needed the feel of hands other than his own on his skin. He headed towards the edge of the woods, he looked around fast, making sure no one else was near, then beckoned the guy forward. Braydon had never initiated an encounter before, and was surprised by the direct and certain steps the young man started taking towards him.

He was a few metres away when Braydon recognized him. Tyra's cousin, Carter. Braydon knew he'd been inside. He almost stopped things then, almost took off fast into the woods, but Carter smiled a small shy smile, and Braydon felt his breath quicken.

They didn't talk. Braydon took Carter's hand and led him into the woods. He pushed him gently against a tree and unzipped Carter's coat, he took off his gloves and slipped one hand into the neck of Carter's shirt and felt his shoulders. He kissed Carter's throat and felt Carter shiver.

Carter and Braydon started meeting up regularly. They didn't go to the cemetery anymore. It was too risky. If Tyra knew what went on up there, she would be devising a scheme. Cameras and blackmail, and, Braydon theorized, eventually using him as bait.

Carter would text Braydon a time and location and Braydon would text back a *Y* or *N*. They didn't talk much, but once Carter had started crying after they had been together and Braydon held him, Carter's big shoulders shook in Braydon's arms. Carter pushed Braydon away after a minute. He pressed the back of both of his hands into his eyes like he could force the tears back in then he walked away.

"Carter," Braydon called after him.

"I'm okay, b'y. I'm okay. I'll see you around," Carter called back.

They hadn't fucked for a while. The weather hadn't been great. Carter borrowed his sister Evie's car once in February, but it didn't feel right, being cooped up in the uncomfortable space. It took all the play out of sex and turned it into a technical operation of fitting their bodies together without bruising themselves on the steering wheel. When they were done, Carter had dropped a used condom out of the car window onto the ground. It felt cheap. They both felt more exposed through the glass of the car windows than hidden out in the woods where tree branches filtered the rest of the world away from them.

Tyra had texted Braydon three times already that morning. Tyra was like a sister to Braydon. Like a sister, he loved her, but he didn't always like her. She was always pushing things too far and, with Cody away, her ideas would snowball out of hand.

Without Cody around, Tyra would suggest breaking into abandoned houses or she would want to start drinking at three in the afternoon, or raiding the medicine cabinet at his parents' house. The last time he was away, Tyra wanted to break into Cody's own house with the key his mom kept under the front mat.

"What for?" Braydon asked her.

"Because we can." Tyra had looked at him with exasperation.

When the text came, Braydon thought it would be Tyra again. But it was from Carter.

~

They were meeting out at a lookout past the beach. There was a spot about half a kilometre from the road, up on the cliffs that overlooked the harbour then beyond out to the ocean proper. A few picnic tables were set up before a track headed up into the woods. Braydon parked by the cove, he pulled the ATV up away from the end of the road and into a spot where it was hidden from view by some alders.

The beach was sheltered, cut out from the land by wind and waves. It was covered in smooth stones and pebbles. Most of the stones were solid grey or grey with dark almost black stripes. A few were red, like old bricks. There were bits of broken white shell with sharp edges and pearly interiors. What little sand there was, was coarse and made up of ground stones. The sand was black where it was wet. It wasn't safe to swim here, there was a wicked undertow, and the sewage outfall was close by. Seagulls bobbed up and down where the pipe came up under the water. The town ended here and gave way to the wilderness. Woods spread out around, and it took only minutes to find yourself completely surrounded by trees. Moose wandered into backyards, and the residents at this end of town could see, from their front-room windows, whales spouting in June and July.

The ice was in now, blocking up the harbour entrance, pans edging up on the shore. A field of white hunks. It was like there were two horizons, one far, far out where the ice met open water, and another just above that where the water met the sky. Fog mist hovered over the ice. When Braydon arrived, there was no sign of Carter. He parked his ATV and breathed in the air. He loved this weather. Everything felt like it was on the edge of something, like you were on a roller coaster and it was just about to tip over the crest of a drop and drag you down. Fog was rolling over the ice, moving like something alive.

There was no wind, and sound seemed to travel faster under the low-lying canopy of cloud. Braydon walked down towards the lookout. The seagulls started making a racket, an eagle rose up from below the cliff edge and a mob of gulls chased it, swooping at it in the air while keeping up their outraged screeching as they drove it from shore. The ice on the surface of the water undulated, slowly and gently, but Braydon knew the ice hunks were heavy. They could crush you if you got caught between them, and if you ended up in the water beneath them it would be almost impossible to push your way out.

He didn't look back down the trail to see if Carter was following him. They had a ritual. They had to keep faith the other would arrive, even if it started raining, or the wind picked up or they had to take an alternative route to their designated meeting place to divert the attention of curious onlookers. Braydon sat on a bench and stared out into the ocean. He shoved his hands in his jacket pockets, felt the cold creeping through the bench seat through his jeans. In the distance he heard a dog barking, then he heard footsteps behind him, but he didn't turn. Carter placed one hand on Braydon's shoulder and squeezed it firmly once before sitting down beside him. Carter was relaxed, his knees gaped open and he leaned forward, loosely clasping his hands together. He didn't look at Braydon, but stared out at the ice.

"It's like the end of the fucking world out here," he said.

They sat listening to bickering seagulls, the dog barking still, and the ice pans jostling each other, pushing against each other as they crowded towards the shore.

~

When Tyra breathed in, she tasted salt and seaweed. She could taste something else too, a hint of funkiness. She had her headphones in. "Bodak Yellow" was playing. Her bike was parked up next to Braydon's ATV, where they always stashed them when they came out here. The high was coming at her, slowly filling up the emptiness she had felt earlier.

Tyra could sense that Braydon had headed down the track, out towards the lookout. She moved along instinctively, like a beagle after a rabbit. She started dancing when she was out of view of the houses. She made her way away from the beach and along the cliff edge that followed the shore, forgetting about Braydon, just enjoying being high.

The polar bear floated in the water. Its head up at the surface, almost indistinguishable from the ice. The bear smelled the gasoline stink of Tyra's dirt bike's engine and the sugariness of her breath. The bear watched her jerking her limbs unnaturally, like she was performing a mating ritual with the rocks around her. The bear was cautious, it thought Tyra might have parasites. The bear could smell something muskier in the distance. A male smell, fresh sweat, sex. This seemed more appetizing than the chemical stench the prey she was watching gave off. The bear raised her snout from the water opened her mouth and took it in, seaweed, smoke from woodstoves, epoxy from the shipyard, deep frying oil, a tutti-frutti–flavoured vape pen. The bear felt the beat that came from the docks, where engines thrummed and, even on Good Friday, a hammer pounded against metal.

Braydon and Carter sat on the bench, they let anticipation build. When Braydon glanced over at Carter's lap, he could see Carter was hard, the crotch of his jeans taut. Braydon's whole body was focused on Carter's, his whole skin primed for Carter's touch, each muscle tense and waiting. He wanted to be in Carter and he wanted Carter in him. He got up from the bench. He had wanted to do this slowly, like he could take it or leave it, but adrenaline made his movement fast. He headed up the trail, he looked back and saw Carter adjust himself, stand then follow him. Once Carter had joined him, they stepped off the trail and pushed into the woods, it felt warmer in there. The green moss beneath their feet was a relief after the grey-scale palette of the shore.

They placed careful footsteps, around boulders and fallen trees, until they were far enough off the trail to be well hidden. Braydon thought about going further in but he was too needy. He needed to touch Carter and feel the muscles underneath his skin. Braydon turned and Carter was right behind him. Braydon placed his hand on the outside of Carter's jeans and felt him. He kissed Carter, softly, then harder. Carter was kissing Braydon back and unfastening his jeans. Braydon knelt before Carter and took him in his mouth. Carter held Braydon by his shoulders his fingers digging in deep, he only grabbed Braydon by the back of his head just before he came and then Braydon took him deep in his throat and Carter threw his head back and groaned.

Braydon spit unceremoniously into the ground beside him. He wiped his mouth with the back of his hand as he stood up and unzipped his jeans ready for Carter to provide him with his own release, excited for Carter's hands around him. They heard an off-key singing in the distance, it lacked tone, but was manic in its enthusiasm. As he recognized Tyra's voice, Braydon felt his erection start to fade.

Braydon and Carter stood still listening to Tyra. They both felt a chill in the air, and Carter shivered. They could tell Tyra was getting closer, heading along the cliff-top path, her voice travelling with force under the canopy of fog they were all under. Then they heard something else, a huffing noise. It was an animal, but not an animal they knew. It wasn't a moose, or the eerie almost human sound of a crying seal. For a moment Braydon thought he had imagined it, then he heard the sound again, a sharp intentional out push of breath, and a snorting.

"What the fuck?" said Carter. Braydon was heading to the forest's edge where he would have a clear view of the cliff-side path. Tyra was still singing or rapping, or whatever she thought she was doing, and the huffing sound happened again.

Carter hauled up his jeans and followed after Braydon.

"Holy fuck," said Braydon, and when Carter reached him, hovering at the edge of the forest, he saw it, the huge white bear, standing on its hind legs, snout in the air breathing in with its mouth open. Ahead of the bear, no more than fifteen metres away, dancing towards them, they saw Tyra. Her earphones were still in. She spun in a circle, her arms outstretched, her eyes closed, her lips moving, her hands together clutching an imaginary mic.

"Tyra!" Braydon screamed. "Tyra!" but she didn't hear him. She was on the cliff path, but also in the stratosphere. Her world glimmered. Her hands rose in the air and she began to twerk, her ass gyrating inexpertly in the direction of the bear.

The bear heard Braydon and looked towards him. The bear took a step towards Tyra, it was a slow step, but Braydon knew how fast those things could move. Even from this distance he could smell the bear: meat breath, saltwater-wet fur, deep musk, the stink of a carnivore.

Braydon was about to dart forward, but he felt Carter's hand on his shoulder, holding him back.

"Wait," Carter said. He was looking around and Braydon saw he was heaving something up, hauling up a hunk of dead tree from the forest floor. It was as tall as Carter was, with branches and dead leaves still attached. Carter picked it up and started heading towards the bear and Tyra. Braydon looked around and picked up his own deadfall. A wind-ruined pine tree, flat on one side, the pine needles brown. It shed needles as he picked it up, but he followed behind Carter the tree held up in the air.

"Tyra," Carter yelled now. He didn't run, he walked slowly, a threatening gait Braydon hadn't seen before. He held his head back, and when Braydon glanced at Carter's face, he saw his eyes were narrowed. Carter watched the bear from the side of his eyes. Like he saw the bear, but it wasn't important enough to garner his full attention.

"Tyra," Braydon screeched, he heard the shake in his voice, but he walked with Carter brandishing the dead tree before him.

Tyra saw them, but didn't understand what they were doing, she thought they were fooling around. She looked curiously at them, two boys playing some silly game with dead wood. Then she recognized Braydon, and her high heart leapt, her feet did too and she skipped towards him, giggling. Braydon her boy, her friend, her very bestie. When Tyra started to move, the bear swung its head fast and dropped down on all fours. Braydon screamed, and Tyra was there before him, she flung her arms around him and the tree he held and tried to get him to spin in a circle with her.

The bear was put off by Tyra's erratic behaviour. The smell had been off from the start, and now it was attacking its own kind. It considered Carter, and his branch. Carter seemed more predator than prey. Taking him down would require effort. The bear longed for the north, for plentiful fat seals.

Carter stood. He held his ground and held his tree up above his head. Tyra clapped her hands, her earphones still in, still oblivious to the bear. The bear moved its head back and forth, looking from Carter to Tyra. Tyra was trying to grab Braydon's hands away from the tree he was clutching. Carter let his tree rest on the ground, and clapped his hands together loudly, stomped his feet and yelled low at the bear like it was a bad dog. "Go! Go home. Get outta here!" The bear backed away a little, then on all fours it started to run back to the beach.

Carter slowly backed up until he was with Tyra and Braydon. He threw down the dead tree grabbed Tyra's upper arms and shook her once fast. She stared at him, her lip pouting, then Carter reached up and took out her earphones. He pointed and it was only then Tyra saw the bear moving away from them and heard its massive paws pounding the ground. Tyra was silent, staring at the bear, like she couldn't quite place what it was. The bear stopped and looked back at them before disappearing from view.

Tyra was having multiple conflicting sensations. She was angry at Carter for shaking her, she was starting to come down, and there was a buzzing sound in her ears that she couldn't get rid of that made everything distorted. She was trying to process the image of the polar bear stuck in her mind, she wanted to ask if Carter and Braydon had seen it, but she didn't want to sound stupid, and then as her brain plummeted and soared, she started grasping at something else: Braydon and Carter, here together, in the woods. She took a step back from them and looked at them both, trying to piece things together.

Braydon's jeans were still undone. He and Carter were standing close together staring at her, they were close enough their bodies were touching casually. Braydon and Cody never stood so close, and then she got it.

Carter lit a smoke and handed it to Braydon, then lit one for himself. Braydon shared his with Tyra without thinking and she dragged on it hard, the nicotine rush ran through her then settled her. They all stared at where the bear had retreated.

Carter had another smoke.

Then they all started cautiously back down the path, towards houses, their rides, town and safety.

All they could hear was silence, until one of the boats in the harbour sounded its horn, calling its crew back.

They stared at the ice floes when they got to the beach, looked hard for the snout of the bear, for signs of the bear swimming in the water. They didn't see her, but she saw them. She lay camouflaged against an ice pan just up the shore, one of her eyes open and fixed on them all.

RESURRECTION

~

Stevie rises again, walking down Water Street early on a Tuesday morning, like a second-rate and unwanted Jesus. It is spring, and more than five years since he died. He looks like he has spent a particularly hard-core weekend out at his cousin's cabin, until the imaginary camera zooms in, then you can see the infestation of beetles clinging to his hair and the white powder crusted on his lips.

Joseph is the first person to see him. He is lifting weights in his living room and sees Stevie walking past his house, through his front window. Joseph never knew Stevie. Knew of him, but he didn't deal with his customers on that level. Stevie looks familiar, but Joseph doesn't make the connection with the picture on the missing posters. The window is a little dirty and he doesn't have his glasses on. He wears contacts when he goes out. He has reached that age, and isn't sure how it happened.

When Kev tried to tell Joseph how he knew the drugs were bad, Joseph stopped him. "I don't need to know about collateral damage," he had said at the time. When he heard Stevie was missing, he had his suspicions it was an overdose, but he was happy not to have them confirmed.

He and Kev still work together on occasional deals. Kev has a legitimate business now too, selling protein powders and athletic gear. It's called Mr. Big's Supplement Store. Kev gave Joseph a two-litre water bottle the last time he stopped by, with Mr. Big's and Kev's logo, a picture of his dog's head, on it.

Joseph observes Stevie and thinks he looks fucked up. He gets closer to the window, watches as he does his reps, makes sure Stevie doesn't pass out in front of the house. The kid looks rough.

Stevie looks through the window and makes eye contact with Joseph. Joseph's guts go cold and he comes out in a sweat, but he shakes it off. He must be dehydrated, pushing himself too hard. He puts down the weights he has been doing scarecrows with, and takes a drink from his water bottle. Maybe he should visit Mr. Big's, and buy some electrolytes.

He shakes his head, puts the image of Stevie in a bubble and sends it away as the new meditative app he has started using tells him to do.

Stevie heads to his mom's house. He lets himself in. Arlene has been making herself a cup of tea with a slug of whisky in it in the kitchen, and comes out into the hallway when she hears the creak of the front door.

"Stevie, Stevie is it you?"

Stevie doesn't speak, he just nods. He sits on the couch and watches her. She brings him tea and toast but he ignores these things. He is not right, she knows. For one thing when he opens his mouth, she can see maggots instead of teeth. There is always this ant walking over his face, crawling over his eyes. And the smell, she doesn't like to mention it, but it's more than just the funk of unwashed clothes that used to hang around him. The smell is something else. He sits for a few days on the couch. He gets up occasionally, walks up to his bedroom, and points to the old milk crate where his Xbox used to stand.

"I gave it away. There was a young boy, with cancer. I met his mom at the church. She said he used it all the time, before..." Arlene doesn't know the polite way to discuss death with her dead son. *Passed* seems inappropriate, as Stevie is passed, but right now is clearly present. Stevie shakes his head. He opens his mouth like he might be moaning, but no sound comes out. Arlene tries to show Stevie the baby picture of him she keeps beside her bed, but Stevie refuses to look at it. He just returns to the couch. When he sits there, he doesn't move. There's no breathing, or the constant fidgeting that Arlene remembers. He's like an ornament. Arlene considers draping something over him, that crocheted tablecloth she never uses. She could do it at night, like you would do with a bird in a cage, but the truth is she doesn't like to get too close to him if she can help it.

"How about a shower, Stevie? Might make you feel better," Arlene suggests, but he ignores her. She had kind of hoped if he stepped in the shower, he might just disintegrate.

Three days after his arrival, she calls and makes an appointment at the doctor's. Arlene makes it under Stevie's name and the receptionist pauses, then says she will be right back she just needs to check in with the doctor. Arlene has never had an appointment so fast. She hates going in, avoided it for years, but after Stevie vanished the minister at her new church got her in, it is all tests and questions. Now she has pills she doesn't take, letters from clinics in St. John's for diagnostic appointments she has no intention of attending.

Stevie comes with her, walks a few steps behind. One of the maggots falls out of his mouth and he bends down to pick it up and pops it back in.

The receptionist recognizes Arlene and tells her to take a seat as soon she walks in the door. Arlene is in one seat and Stevie's beside her. The chairs are hard plastic. There are no magazines anymore to flip through and distract yourself from the poster on the wall with a picture of toenail fungus. You just have to sit with your own thoughts until you are allowed through to your appointment. The doctor comes out after hardly a minute. Beckons Arlene into the examination room, and somehow Stevie slips away. He's just gone. He must have slipped out the front door of the clinic, but Arlene didn't hear anything. The doctor is concerned, asks Arlene if she has been drinking. How often she sees Stevie. Is she taking her medication? "You were the only one in the waiting room, Arlene." The doctor places a gloved but concerned hand on Arlene's forearm.

Arlene is pissed off, but she plays along. She knows Stevie's sudden appearance is inconvenient as it disrupts the usual way of things, but she can't help that. "I must have been mistaken," she concurs. "Not been getting much sleep." Arlene knows what's going on behind the doctor's mask, she's walking through the steps of calling up the Waterford, setting up an assessment. "Do you have someone you can get to come stay with you for a while?"

"Yes," Arlene says, but she doesn't. The doctor seems more capable of accepting this unreality than the reappearance of Arlene's son. There are different ways of knowing things, that is one thing Arlene knows for sure.

There is a stench to Arlene's couch she can't get rid of. She soaks the couch in Febreze, and eventually flips the cushion over. She takes out one of Stevie's school photos and sticks it on top of her TV. She gets some holy water from Jackie, who cleans the priest's house, and splashes it around. When Jackie asks her what it's for, Arlene says, "Best you don't know." Jackie accepts this.

Evie is headed out the door, heading to her class in St. John's. Stevie is standing by her car. She stops, the smell of him hits her first, before she sees him.

"Stevie?" she asks. He cocks his head at her and sort of smiles, and out bubble a few maggots. Evie knows Stevie is real and not real.

"You want something, Stevie?" Evie asks. "I'm sorry. I'm sorry for what happened to you."

Stevie opens his mouth and a butterfly flies out. It lands, for a moment, on the windshield of Evie's car. Her eyes take it in, it is all gold and blue and not of this place. She looks up at Stevie and he has vanished, she looks back for the butterfly and it is gone too.

Cody and Tyra see Stevie. They took some pills earlier in the day, and then watched animal-attack videos until lunch. Tyra's been obsessed recently, keeps making Cody watch this woman get bitten by a polar bear at the Berlin Zoo, that one is PG compared to most of what she watches. She will google anything. Man Killed by Alligator, Pit Bull Kills Toddler. They are headed out to the store to get chips when they see Stevie, and Tyra starts laughing, and insulting him. "Look at you, b'y. What do you think this is, *The Walking Dead?*"

Cody is terrified. He runs away, he turns back once and sees Tyra running towards Stevie, throwing rocks at him. The rocks fly right through him. He continues to come towards Tyra and she plants herself on the sidewalk in front of him. "I'm not afraid of you," she screams at him. He walks right through her, but when he's there and she's inside of him, he stops. She can't move, she can't breathe, she's suffocating.

She wakes up flat out on the sidewalk with Shannon from the store hanging over her, "You alright, girl? I'm calling your nan." Tyra sits up with Shannon's help, brushes a beetle off her cheek.

Ryan gets off work at three. He showers, and heads out to walk the trails. He's not very far in, not even in the woods yet. There is a memorial bench for Stevie that looks out over the water, and when Ryan gets to it, Stevie is sitting on the bench looking at the ocean. When Ryan gets to him, Stevie pats the bench beside him, and despite the long curling nails Ryan sees on Stevie's hand he sits down beside him, and together they look out over the water. The water shimmers and moves, a whale breaches not too far offshore. It's the first one he has seen this year, an early visitor. "Look at that, Stevie," Ryan says, and looks at Stevie. Stevie points to where the whale breached, and Ryan sees a group of fish, but it's not capelin, it's tropical fish, in blue and yellow and green and they're floating around on top of the water, flying around like starlings, not like fish at all. He blinks and they are gone and so is Stevie. Instead of heading up into the woods he walks back towards town. He sends a text to Evie.

what r u doing later? want to get a coffee?

He adds a smiling cat with heart eyes emoji, sends it, then worries it is too much. But Evie's reply comes fast.

sounds good

Ryan feels elated.

Kev is at the store, ready to close up. They close at eight but it has been a quiet evening. Truth is, the store is never that busy. His dog, Skeeter, is lying on the floor, and Kev is looking over the day's cash taking. Figuring out how much dirty money he can get away with cleaning today. He'll talk to Joseph, see if he can do a discreet pickup of the expired powder and figure out how to make it look like sales. He hears Skeeter whining. "Hang on, buddy, my good boy. Daddy's almost done here." Usually this does the trick, but Skeeter keeps whining and Kev looks up, and there's Stevie standing in the store. Kev blinks, usually this makes Stevie go away, but not today. Stevie remains, looking around.

"Look, buddy, we're closed," Kev says. "Open tomorrow, at eleven, provided Cody shows up on time."

Stevie puts his hands over his head and shakes them around, all of his fingers fall off and hit the floor and start slithering away. Skeeter chases one and gets it in his mouth.

"Drop it." Skeeter opens his mouth and drops the finger at Kev's command. It starts sliding across the floor back to Stevie and then it reattaches itself, the other fingers are all returning to him, slowly. Stevie's head flops from side to side and he watches as his hand reassembles.

Kev starts to cry then. He sits behind his desk and puts his head on his hands. Skeeter comes over and puts his head on Kev's lap. Kev feels a slight pressure on his own head, and realizes Stevie is petting him, just like he is petting Skeeter. Kev lets out a sob and Skeeter barks three times, and then Stevie is gone.

Susie wakes up and Stevie is in bed beside her. His eyes are open. One of the cats is lying on top of him, batting him occasionally, swatting at an insect that runs over his face. Susie looks at him then gets up. She's seen Stevie before, she is almost used to him. He stays in bed with the cat when she feeds the dog, but when she gets out of the shower, he's sitting on the toilet. She covers herself up quickly with a towel. She wasn't going to go for a run, but with Stevie hanging around she won't get much painting done, so she pulls on her running clothes. Stevie follows her out the door. He jogs behind her, she can't hear him breathing or any footfall, but when she turns around, he's there, a few feet behind her. It's making her run faster. Her lungs are burning, but she keeps going.

ACKNOWLEDGEMENTS

Earlier versions of some of these stories appeared in the following literary magazines. "That Running Girl" appeared in *Riddle Fence* Issue no. 25 (2016). "We Smoke Our Smokes" appeared in *Geist* Issue no. 110 (2018). "Vigil" was Second Runner-up for the 2020 *PRISM international* Jacob Zilber Prize for Short Fiction and appeared in *PRISM international* Issue no. 58.4 that year. "Stevie Dies Twice" was published in *The Fiddlehead* Issue no. 283 (2020), and "Bang, Bang, Bang" (originally titled "Do You Know Who I Am, B'y?") appeared in *Geist* Issue no. 118 (2021). I am indebted to these magazines and their editors for their care and for supporting my writing.

I am grateful for the financial support I received from the Canada Council for the Arts and from the Newfoundland and Labrador Arts Council while working on this project.

Thanks to everyone at Breakwater Books: the amazing Rebecca Rose and everyone who works so hard to turn manuscripts into books.

Thanks to my editor, Kate Kennedy, who just gets it and who knows how to make stories stronger, and to my copy editor, Shelley Egan, for putting up with my complete hopelessness around hyphens.

The writers Sharon Bala, Diane Carley, Eva Crocker, Chloe Edbrooke, Carmella Gray-Cosgrove, and Tracey Waddleton gave me feedback on these stories, in various forms, over the past nine years. Thank you to you all.

Carmella has read too many versions of this manuscript, puts up with my badly composed texts, and lets me hang out with her beautiful family. Our friendship is one of the greatest gifts writing has given me.

Diane and Sarah, Peg and Gerry, and all the other fabulous and fabulously queer folk of Small Point-Adam's Cove-Blackhead-Broad Cove—and my friends in Harbour Grace—thanks for filling my life with joy and constant inspiration. This book is not about Harbour Grace, but she is my muse and I love her.

To the Hotel Estoril Eden, and the solitude I found there, for making Kev, Stevie, and all the other b'ys come alive.

Mum, Sam, Captain Jack, Madonna, and Roxy for looking after me. The late great Poppy Cat, for sitting on my lap for most of these first drafts.

Colleen Soulliere, you talk about the characters in this book as if they are real people, you believe in me when I don't, and despite the fact I think you are too hard on Kev, I value your opinion over all others. Thank you for coming home every day to unknown moods brought on by literary weather and for building this life with me. I am just so damn lucky to be with you.

Susie Taylor (she/her) is a queer writer living in rural Newfoundland. Her first novel, *Even Weirder Than Before*, was published in 2019 by Breakwater Books. Taylor's short stories have appeared in *Geist*, *Prism International*, *The Fiddlehead*, *Room Magazine*, *Riddle Fence* and elsewhere. Taylor lives in Harbour Grace, Newfoundland and Labrador, with her partner and two cats. When she isn't writing, she is out running.